CW01617650

SILVER MOON

GREAT NOVELS
OF
EROTIC DOMINATION
AND
SUBMISSION

NEW TITLES EVERY MONTH

www.smbooks.co.uk

TO FIND OUT MORE ABOUT OUR READERS' CLUB
TO FIND OUT MORE ABOUT OUR READERS' CLUB WRITE TO;

SILVER MOON READER SERVICES;
Hexgreave Hall
Farnsfield
Nottinghamshire NG22 8LS
Tel; 01157 141616

YOU WILL RECEIVE A FREE MAGAZINE OF EXTRACTS FROM OUR EXTENSIVE RANGE OF EROTIC FICTION ABSOLUTELY FREE. YOU WILL ALSO HAVE THE CHANCE TO PURCHASE BOOKS WHICH ARE EXCLUSIVE TO OUR READERS' CLUB

***

NEW AUTHORS ARE WELCOME

Please send submissions to;
Barrington Hall Publishing
Hexgreave Hall
Farnsfield N22 8LS

SILVER MOON

PRESENTS

HOW TO SPANK A WOMAN

BY

PETER PRINCE

VOLUME I: PUNISHMENT TECHNIQUES

CONTENTS:

INTRODUCTION

Do your girl's feet twitch too much for your liking when you slipper her pretty bottom? Perhaps you are unsure how hard and how frequent her canings should be, or you wish to safely and intimately interrogate her so that you can enjoy wringing even the most closely guarded secrets from her quivering breast. Maybe you desire to more closely control her arousal and sexual secretions during discipline, or you just need a few pointers on elegant use of the male erection to maximise female discomfort and chagrin during lengthy punishment.

Whatever tools you require to pin that wriggling wench down firmly beneath your sadistic thumb, you will find them here in this, the modern bible of bare bottom beating. It is the definitive dictionary of domestic domination and an essential primer for every persecutor of a pink and pouting pudendum.

In a genre crowded with stories that are sometimes difficult to tell apart, this highly original work stands alone in both the depth of its eroticism and the beauty of its prose. It is a lovingly crafted guide to the sexual chastisement of women, written from the perspective of a real English gentleman, exploring every secret of his licentious subject matter with an enthralling blend of rigorous factual detachment and indulgent, lustful fervour.

This series of deliciously explicit and fascinating confessions paints an exciting picture of the expert sexual punishment techniques of a very refined and profoundly dominant man, completely at home in the modern, liberated world. Written with compassion and wit, it describes in enthusiastic, poetic and often minute detail the ordeals to which he subjects his willing and submissive female consorts for the inseparable purposes of their discipline and his sensual arousal.

It covers the delights of traditional bare bottom caning etiquette, effective and vigorous over-the-knee spanking methods, the Japanese secrets of female genital procedures, as well as the most satisfying way to beat a girl in the interests of keeping her fit and healthy. It is the truly definitive guide to the dos and don'ts of the most noble pursuit of pleasurable and practical power over your willing sub as she quivers irresistibly in submissive heat.

Quite simply anyone who enjoys perusing beautiful prose, and whipping a maiden's delectable derriere until she squeals, will just love this book and read it many times. It is not only an indispensable guide for any man wishing to learn how to express his masterful side, but is required reading for cultured men and women who crave wonderful stories and detailed descriptions of erotic corporal punishment.

A Health Warning:

If you have now, or at any time in the past, suffered from any kind of serious medical condition, please consult your doctor before reading this book. I cannot be held responsible for cardiac arrests, strokes or any form of babbling delirium induced by the unbearably sensual nature of the material in this volume.

I apologise to anyone whose constitution is not strong enough to enjoy these irresistibly vivid accounts of the most mind-blowing erotic disciplinary practices and incredible sexual adventures. That's just the way it is, and you're going to have to miss out on something that would have enriched your presumably quite short life immeasurably.

Sorry.

Peter Prince.

CANE YOUR GIRL WITH CONFIDENCE: PART 1

In Part 1 I shall describe the basics and benefits of regularly caning your wench, the finer points of the perfect bottom-whipping stroke, and generally revel in the delightful aspects of exposing a girl's rear end to this truly wonderful and terrifying instrument of female punishment.

WHY CANE HER?

For many years, I have been the proud owner of a classic school cane, and when I am blessed by the constant companionship of a submissive female, it is my great pleasure to use it with regularity and real enthusiasm upon her bare, twitching bottom. Sometimes this is to punish her girly misdeeds, often merely to satisfy my manly lust to whip her naked body, and occasionally just to remind her which one of us is really in charge.

Of course, I also beat her until she squirms more frequently with other, lesser implements, and I am especially fond of tanning her naked cheeks with either an old-fashioned wooden ruler – affectionately named the "Pussy Whacker" – or a regulation issue school plimsoll, reinforced with a heavy wooden insole.

These two kinder instruments of rear end retribution are actually more recreational than correctional, in my view. I frequently pin her soft tail over my knee in the bedroom, or more often in my study, and take down her knickers to wallop seven bells out of her with the Pussy Whacker, either because I am bored, maybe feeling sexy, or have just plain had a hard day and want to let off some steam by whacking her long and hard while she wriggles and yells for my amusement.

The plimsoll, too, has its place as one of my favoured toys, but that is more often reserved for longer, more humiliating spankings at the end of one of our special games: competitive activities in which she inevitably ends up as the loser (and a sore one at that!)

In a later chapter, I shall outline the principles of these fixed outcome pursuits, in which she inescapably earns a bottom whipping for finishing second, since they are an excellent means for reinforcing her inferior standing in our home, whilst simultaneously providing a failsafe excuse for painfully skinning her delicious derriere.

But if these sexy whackings are the hors d'oeuvres and gravy of our spankingly wonderful love life together, then the meat and potatoes are surely the strict and formal canings that I love to subject her to, the mere threat of which can set her aflutter in that tummy tingling way that only a really, very naughty girl can understand.

It's difficult to explain our deep and profound emotional relationship with the cane to any man who hasn't ever used one to beat upon the naked hindquarters of his lovely girl, but let me try to share with you something of the wonders conjured up by the marvellous phenomenon that is a bare bottom caning.

WHAT MAKES THE CANE SO SPECIAL?

People who've never actually seen or felt a classic school cane often imagine it to be some kind of walking stick, or perhaps something rather like a garden cane for runner beans. This is quite wrong.

The first astonishing thing you notice about a school cane (that is how I like to refer to my preferred punishment cane since it is used primarily to teach her important lessons) is how surprisingly light it is. It's as easy to pick up as a biro, and about the same thickness, and for an object just over two and a half feet long, that makes it seem too flimsy to inflict real pain. It's also incredibly flexible, and can be bent into a complete circle with no strength whatsoever.

You might imagine that these properties make the hallowed rod virtually useless for delivering authentic punishment. Nothing could be further from the truth. In that apparent and wholly illusory softness, lies the special magic of the cane. That supple, feather light, bamboo staff is a device designed precisely to inflame controlled agony when applied quickly and with skill across the bare cheeks of a properly presented female behind.

An unbroken lineage of a thousand years, perhaps more, of uninterrupted woman whipping, have produced through trial and error, this modern masterpiece of posterior torment technology.

The school cane is designed specifically and beautifully to punish the naughty girl's bottom, and none should ever doubt its power, precision and truly pussy tingling menace. It turns even the most timid master into an icon of terrifying male power: a man who requires and receives both submission and worship from his wench.

I once used to cane a girl who said that having her bottom and fanny just tapped by its light tip, made her clitoris feel like it was about to explode, so much did she dread the first delightful stroke as her bare hips gently bounced with uncontainable anxiety.

"I get so worked up, I think I'm going to piss!" she confided, touchingly.

STRIPING HER BOTTOM

As he stands aroused above her bare and quivering tail, a girl's master holds in his hands an artefact that can, with the minimum use of force, create almost unlimited fiery pain in her exposed and separated cheeks without causing one single permanent score, nor breaking the skin of even the most sensitive naked rear.

I have caned squaws with highly responsive bottoms, which, though often beautifully marked, remained permanently unscarred and still deliciously twitchy, despite the countless lengthy and expert sessions I used to make them endure over my whipping stool.

In fact, a proper caning, delivered with skill, loving care and unbending intent to punish, will leave only a very attractive, temporary set of red tramlines, spaced at the intervals desired by the caner across the entire width of her buttocks (and thighs if desired). This tattooing is comely evidence of a properly punished bottom, and should be worn with pride as it gradually fades from even the palest complexion over the course of a week or so.

A girl proudly adorned with such clear evidence of expertly delivered discipline can with a single flash of her bare arse, declare silently to the world:

"My master knows how to beat me properly."

As well as these lovely thin red lines, there will be darker, deeper marks where the very tip of the cane makes harsher contact with her bare bottomflesh, a bit like the end of a cracking whip. These exceptionally painful scorches are called "bitemarks" and gaining sufficient control of the rod to avoid them if desired, or apply them to precise points on her bottom, is a mark of a very accomplished caner.

Indeed, the unique flexibility of the school cane makes it possible for very advanced adepts to inflict accurate bites actually between her buttocks both above and below her anus. To receive these unbearable stings, the girl must ensure that her cheeks are held high and well separated and some

adjustment of the angle of the punisher's caning stance may be necessary, depending on the skill of the beater and the depth of the chastisee's bottom cleavage.

Having a naughty girl's bare bottom and vulva spread wide upon a silver platter and awaiting your precise and wrathful pleasure in this way, is guaranteed to stiffen even the most monumental whipping erection. To calm your feverish excitement a little, and thus prevent mistaken cane bites landing directly upon the wench's desperately pouting anus and labia, I recommend an enjoyable pause during which you apply stern finger pressure to the exact and intimate points of her anatomy that you intend to set aflame with your carefully targeted canetip.

This will allow you to steady your no doubt trembling hands, whilst simultaneously increasing the anxiety tensions in her tummy, legs, vagina and bottom cheeks, as she struggles to keep them in position for you while knowing in advance exactly where each hackle raising scorch is going to land among the private places of her tender bottom.

Correctly achieved, these waspish little bud burns hurt like the devil on horseback, so you will need to apply bites to these special hotspots sparingly and with great care. But it is a great flourish with which to finish a memorable beating: an accomplished painter of shivering pain, signing his quivering canvas with a bamboo quill.

"Let's have that arse high and wide, now girl, I want to be able to see right up that bottom. You'll remember the end of this lesson the next time you scratch your tail, my little pussycat."

Being a very committed caning enthusiast, I usually demand to closely inspect my sub's backside daily, whenever she is over my knee for her recreational spankings or regular vaginal massage sessions, to ensure that the caning tramlines and bites that I value so highly are always present.

Fresh bites in very sensitive places can be pressed hard or pinched either to see how much they still hurt, or simply to recreationally humiliate and torment her. In any event, it certainly would not do for a man of my rank to possess a wench with an unmarked rear, and when her punishment burns are deemed too faint, it is time to refresh them, inventing a reason to fetch her to the whipping stool if necessary. (Though, prone as girls are to frequent laziness and casual insolence these days, such creativity is rarely called for.)

The school cane is the perfect tool for any man to use to subdue the modern, wilful girl, because its unique agony-magnifying properties mean that even those males of somewhat lesser physical strength have much greater leverage over her distress while relishing a slow and proper beating.

And if your female has been gradually and patiently trained to withstand a severe arse warming, and since you can swing it satisfyingly hard with no risk of injury to her naked tail, this makes it an appropriate implement to administer heated, angry thrashings as well as cold, calculated sets of measured and excruciating whacks.

THE SWEET SOUNDS OF A CANING

Its extreme lightness and flexibility also combine to give rise to another deeply erotic property: the exciting sound that it makes while being used upon her.

The school cane produces two beautiful and very distinct noises. There is the voluminous “whoosh”, or deep, full-bodied “whistle”, as the stalk is swung hard and fast through the air. This gushing whoop is the audible emissary of tail-end agony, heralding the heated arrival of the dreaded stroke itself. Even if her bottom is safely encased in both her thong and skintight jeans, when she hears you taking private practice swipes, it will make her knees tremble to listen at your study door.

It's what girls like to call a "wet-knicker noise".

Then there is the sharper impact sound, known as the "whop", "whack" or "crack". All three terms describe different aspects of the whipping noise as the thin and hollow rod makes contact with the thick flesh of her sweet bottom, but no single word actually does it justice alone. A presenting girl, hearing that delectable sound has just enough time to register the strangely gentle sensation of impact before the waves of goose-pimpling agony explode through and envelop her submissively raised hindquarters, filling her taut backside seemingly forever with glorious fire, from pouting bud to tingling clit. Ding dong.

I always cane my girl in my study, and one of the many very good reasons for this is that the sparse furnishings of that stern chamber create much more satisfying acoustics to enhance the beating. Such a close echo really magnifies both the whistle and whack of the cane as well as her whimpers, yelps and cries, as she has the sin seared mercilessly from her hapless, wriggling tail.

This always helps to provide a far more formal and erotic ambience for her caning punishments than it is ever possible to achieve in the bedroom, where her daily hand, ruler and plimsoll paddlings are lovingly applied to her fit back end.

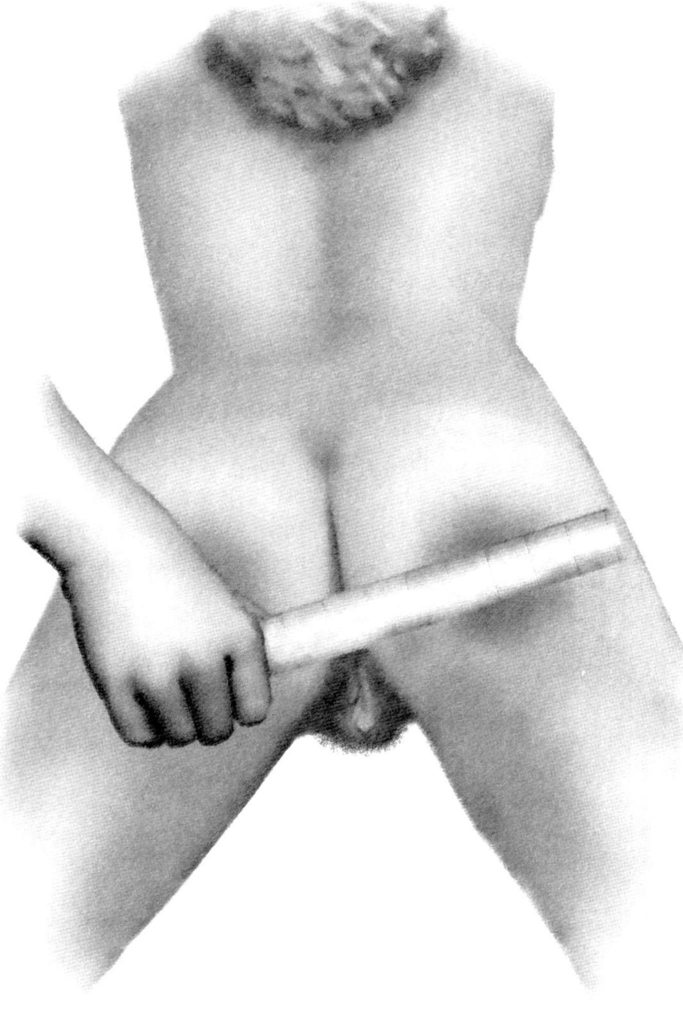

THE MAGIC OF THE CANE

I simply love my cane, and my wench both worships and adores it, as she does me. Thus, the intense almost spiritual emotions summoned up by this relationship between the three of us – my little minx, her deified master and his beloved school cane – give rise to an additional, natural sense of ritual and precision to the whippings I enjoy visiting upon her soft and yielding nether regions.

The cane is, in short, a miraculous thing. A gift of wonder and a magic wand. We should not question the reasons for its existence, but simply give thanks to the God of Punishment for its supernatural punishment power.

In part 2, I shall describe in detail the precise art of applying the cane to the bare bottom of a properly submitted wench to maximise both the disciplinary effectiveness of the punishment, and the sexual pleasure you derive from visiting it upon her shapely female rear.

CANE YOUR GIRL WITH CONFIDENCE: PART 2

In part 1, I introduced the cane as the ultimate implement with which to instil obedience into even the feistiest female minx. In this second disciplinary instalment, I intend to describe how I like to put the art and science of a bamboo beating into practice. A big thank-you to all the willing wenches, and their devoted bottoms, who have submitted to my excruciating experimentations over the years.

PROMISING HER A BEATING

I think it is important to choose one's words carefully, when informing a girl that she is about to be caned. This allows a frequently whipped wench to tell how angry I am, simply by the way I invoke the blessed whipping rod by name:

"I'm going to beat some manners into your naked bottom with the cane, young lady."

Versus:

"I'm going to cane some sense into your bare arse, you naughty little bitch!"

My tone can be soft and menacing, or cold and strict, and after a few dozen thrashings, she should be able guess how many strokes she is likely to receive on the basis of that alone.

Six of the best is the basic unit of traditional punishment, of course, but she usually gets at least two sets, making twelve, but it could be anything up to twenty four for a long, drawn out beating. And I like to take my time.

But no matter how angry I am, or how turned on, there is always that rigorous formality to my caning routine, a rigidity of form reflected in the throbbing hardness of my cock as she obediently goes about preparing herself as best she can to be whipped.

STRIPPING HER FOR WHIPPING

She has to undress first, in front of me. This is usually done in the study, where the caning is to be given; so that she will feel most uncomfortable and embarrassed stripping naked in what is effectively an office environment.

I can sit back in my chair behind my desk, liberate and stroke my straining manhood, or simply watch her over steepled fingers. I like to maximise her humiliation with my wicked smile, and direct her to carefully fold and put away her clothes under a small chair in the corner. She has to bend over with her back to me to do this and when she straightens up to look at me, she sees me grinning from ear to ear, delighted by the private display to which I have just been treated.

Then, naked and flushing hot with shame and excitement (and shame at my excitement, as she stands there in bare-bottomed silence looking anxiously at the rampant, pulsing bone I have released from my fly) she must wait while I decide whether or not to make her wear the t-shirt.

You see, sometimes I like her to be totally naked for a caning, and at other times I prefer her bare arse, pussy and legs to be framed by a special t-shirt that I've had made especially for these wonderful occasions. It is tight fitting, of course and too short to cover even her navel. It's white with big black letters on the front that read "Whipping Girl" and a smaller script on the back that says "Beat Here" with an arrow pointing down to her exposed derrière.

So it's the birthday suit or the whipping girl vest: either costume is guaranteed to shame her to the core.

It is also my occasional pleasure to insist upon the wearing of a pair of spotless, white socks. There's something delightfully innocent and helpless about the way they bob pleasingly up and down as her little feet kick in desperate synchrony with her pointless struggle to contain the suffering that each of my leisurely strokes effortlessly ignites within her helpless, and semi-naked form.

And as she dons them at my command, pulling them carefully up the smooth skin of her calves, folding the tops to be neat and straight, while she treats me to another bent over display of her female secrets, she knows that she is doing this for my satisfaction, that I might enjoy the whipping of her all the more.

Though I am not a fussy man by any means, I find it is these little touches, these small, attractive and debasing garnishes around the banquet of her punishment that transform the joyful beating of a girl into an ecstasy beyond description.

SHAMING HER THOROUGHLY

When I'm good and ready, I stand up slowly, completely in control of both her and the situation. My released erection testifies to my electric pleasure, and I'm in no hurry. Apart from that blatant and very dominant exposure, I am completely clothed in contrast to her own very vulnerable, naked bottom.

I love to pat and admire her exposed hips and taut bum. To me, my woman's naked thighs and buttocks are special symbols of my power over her, and to have to flaunt them in front of me like that always humbles her, and excites me even further. My bare cock is like iron.

It is my habit to saunter over to her, getting right up close so that she dares not look me in the eye. I can scent her, and her deep and rich aroma betrays how aroused she is by her predicament.

"Smells like you're in heat again, bitch. We'll have to beat that out of you."

If she's wearing the t-shirt, I like to carefully straighten and smooth it, or if she's completely bare, I might just tickle my hands over her breasts and shoulders, and run my finger quickly up between her naked bottom cheeks, making her jump, or even better, cry out in alarm.

I know my hard-on always embarrasses her when she's being punished, and I love to draw her attention to it either by pressing it against her hips, bottom or mons, or even taking her hand and guiding it up the full length of my pulsing shaft.

Then it's time for a prophetically sharp slap across the buns as I command her: "Get your bare arse over there and fetch me the whipping stool!"

BEAT
HERE

THE WHIPPING STOOL

Our special stool lives in the corner of my study and it is utterly fabulous. It's a square topped bar stool, which I've customised: about three feet tall with an upholstered seat that I've padded at one side to give a gentle slope of about 30 degrees.

When the stool is placed in the middle of the room next to my desk, it leaves enough space for me to comfortably swing my right arm, cane in hand. I like to pat the padded seat and order her into position.

"Get your bare pussy over the whipping stool, girl!" is one of my favourite orders. "Assume the position, wench!" is another. Sometimes it's nice to give her another full and firm slap on the rear and smile: "Let's have that bottom in the air, shall we?"

She can bend over it quite comfortably, so that her feet are off the ground and her bottom is propped up very provocatively by the thicker edge of the seat. Her rear points up nicely, at just the right angle to make a fine target and give the cane strokes maximum penetration into her tender tail.

With her arse in this most attractive position, the blows can be delivered easily and cleanly: either flat and direct, angled slightly downward, or most cutting of all, with a slight upward curve at the last minute. I'm capable of performing all these variations with stunning accuracy, having had frequent opportunities to perfect my technique.

If I do feel it necessary to tie her down there's a specially fitted belt under the seat that can be fastened round the small of her back to pin her waist. Additionally, the lower crossbars provide excellent attachment points for her wrists at the front, and her knees can be roped to the stool legs and mid bars at each side at the back, to restrain her inevitable kicking reflex during the beating and to hold her hips a suitable distance apart.

SEPARATING HER CHEEKS

This double binding simultaneously pushes her quim out temptingly behind so that it peeps enticingly from between her parted thighs for ease of tweaking with fingers, tapping with the cane, or for when I get too excited, plunging my twitching bone into, either for a few calming thrusts, or even to completely discharge the boiling contents of my straining testes, should the punishment be nearing its natural and climactic end.

But whatever penetrative endeavours it subsequently inspires, I find that the sight and perfume of the female pudenda always excites me to beat with a more delighted enthusiasm. It puts a smile on the face of even my most determined fury while I whip those quivering cheeks until I come.

Bound or not, it's very important to me that those cute buttocks of hers should be kept well separated during a caning. This is not merely because I need easy access to her pussy for the purposes of vigorous entry and torment, and to her bum crack for targeting with my expert "biting" strokes. (See Part 1 for a discussion on the art of using the cane tip to safely and accurately mark sensitive parts of her bottom)

No, my view is that not only are the female buttocks more attractive when taut and splayed, but you can also tell a great deal about the efficacy of a beating by its effects on your girl's anus. With this in mind, I closely monitor the pouting and clenching of her nether bud during and after the application of each stroke and increase the fierceness if necessary to provoke it to a more powerful and satisfying twitch of reflex agony.

My feeling is that a proper stroke should be painful enough to produce a pronounced involuntary contraction of the anus that I call a "pink kiss". If she doesn't show me a decent pink kiss, then the whack doesn't count and will have to be repeated until she does. Needless to say, she works hard at providing this attractively intimate action as spectacularly as she can.

TEASING HER PRIVATES

Of course, not just as her doting master, but also simply as a red-blooded man, I am perpetually fascinated by the nooks and crannies of her bottom. Whenever I have her vulnerable end in an accessible configuration, I always want to engage in some tactile exploration of her naked privates prior to her punishment, "just to check the smoothness of the waxing" I like to tease.

So having been told to "assume the position" she must climb onto the whipping stool and clamp her knees against the wooden legs to separate her cheeks and await the cold tickle of my prying fingertips.

I may sometimes help her to open her thighs by pushing the undercurves of her bottom apart with my palms. This exerts an uncomfortable tension upon her anus and opens her pussy embarrassingly wide, making it easy to insert my thumbs into her for an even more unbearable stretch.

A minute or two of this ends with a good, hard smack, letting her know that she must keep her secrets as open as she can to endure the next few endless moments of affectionate torment.

I like a girl to have a very ticklish bottom, especially up and down between the cheeks, and I make it my business to know every special personal weakness of her sensitive rear end just so that I can ruthlessly exploit her vulnerability at times like these. I often tease, jiggle, pinch, poke, prod and tweak her like that until her thighs are pumping and her pussy is twitching before laughing at her helpless squirms and giving her upturned rear a condescending pat.

"Don't make such a fuss, girl. I haven't even started to beat you, yet!"

I can change her mood from frustration to fear instantly by saying:

"Let's get down to business."

It's a phrase that chills her pink, tickled, hairless tail to a cold sweat in a moment.

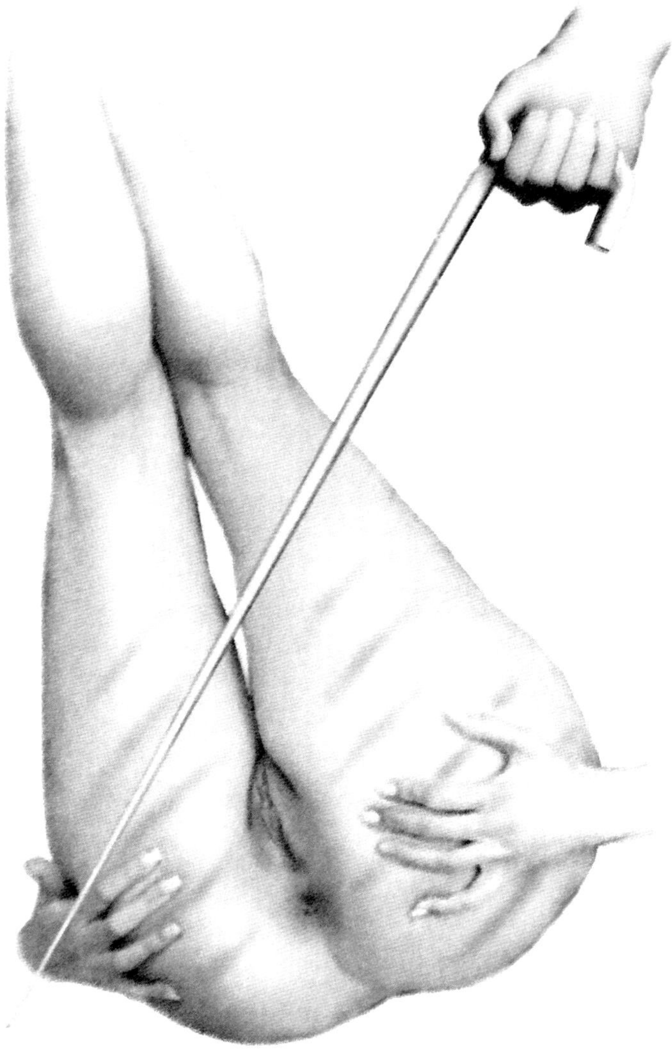

WARMING UP THE CANE

I like to fetch the cane myself, while she's in position over the stool and able to watch me retrieve the whipping stick from behind the study door. I love to measure its length in front of her, flex it, tap my palm with it and then look at her. I gleefully point out to her how the wood is seasoned in places – made darker by the stains of painsweat from her bottom and pussymilk spattered from her bucking quim - glancing along the naked length of her to measure and savour the work I am about to undertake and enjoy.

One girl loved to tell me it was like having a screw tightened in her belly, and this unbearable anxiety will often force a naked squaw to gasp quietly, and kick her legs a little, as though struggling in anticipation of the beating to come. But I'm nowhere near done teasing her.

As I have explained at length, school canes are very whippy, and it is my custom to take loud and vicious practice swipes through the air, both in front of her face and then, terrifyingly, behind her bottom. Each piercing whistle makes her buttocks clench and quiver, and her pussy lift involuntarily. Eventually I just tap her bare cheeks lightly with the tip of the cane:

"I want them taut but not tight, young lady. Taut but not tight. Lift those feet a little."

By making her raise her feet up and out somewhat, I can get her bottom nice and firm, just as I like to beat it, and keep her cheeks spread to the extent that I desire. This action makes her feel so open and exposed; she's offering me her softest places to do with as I cruelly please.

I use the cane itself to let her know whether her postural exertions are pleasing me adequately:

"Good!" will get her a gentle whack, just enough to make

her jump. "More!" will earn her a sharp canespank across the privates, sending waves of aching fire up from her open twat, prompting her to quickly fulfil my brusque command.

I have just one more little game to play, before commencing punishment. My own chair has a large, flat cushion on it, and I place this seat in front of her, and take powerful practice whacks at it while I describe to her the beating she is about to receive. A cane makes a truly frightening noise when it's whopped against a soft surface like that, especially when she's naked, cringing and presented over a whipping stool, awaiting her bottom-scorching, just desserts.

"I've been looking forward to this all day." WHOP!

"I'm going to flay the skin off your bare arse, girl." WHOP!

"I'm going to beat you until your pussy twitches." WHOP! WHOP! WHOP!

And so forth.

Then I take up position behind her. We have a big mirror on one side of the room that allows her to see both of us while she lies poised in that undignified waiting position. This means that she can see for herself how my eyes remain fixed on her lovely bottom throughout the punishment, watching like a hawk for those pink kisses, inspecting the tramlines and bitemarks as they emerge, loving my work and dizzying in her squeaks.

I occasionally meet her gaze in the mirror with a delighted smile as I inhale the musky aroma of her aroused and fearful perspiration, milked from her private places and ready to be flung into the air by the graceful arcs of my perfect caning swipes.

Finally ready to begin whipping her, I take the opportunity to lay down some ground rules for the beating:

"Don't you dare move while I'm caning the living daylights out of your bare arse, you little minx. Twitch your legs all you want, but if you shift that bottom an inch you'll earn yourself another six, girl"

"I'm damn angry with you, and I want to hear some squealing today."

MAKING HER HOWL APPROPRIATELY

Now that command always hides a double-edged threat. Though she is allowed to yell out "Ouch!" or "Ow!" or even "Youch!" or "Oooh" before she enumerates the stroke for me, too much easy yelping and screaming is deemed self-indulgent and will earn her extra strokes.

No, it is my oft stated philosophy that the demeanour of a girl enduring the cane should be one of quiet desperation, and that she ought to make every effort to swallow her anguish and gasp, groan and choke in a stifled and contained fashion while she is being punished. I might even give her a pencil to bite down on if I really mean to go to town on her tormented backside.

That's not to say that I don't want her to howl. Oh no. I want noise, but I also greatly enjoy the process of working up a sweat by forcing her to wail. Young women are deliciously prone to vocalise their distress in a most delightful fashion, and let me assure you all that though she does her level best to keep a lid on it, she will always end up shrieking at the top of her lungs.

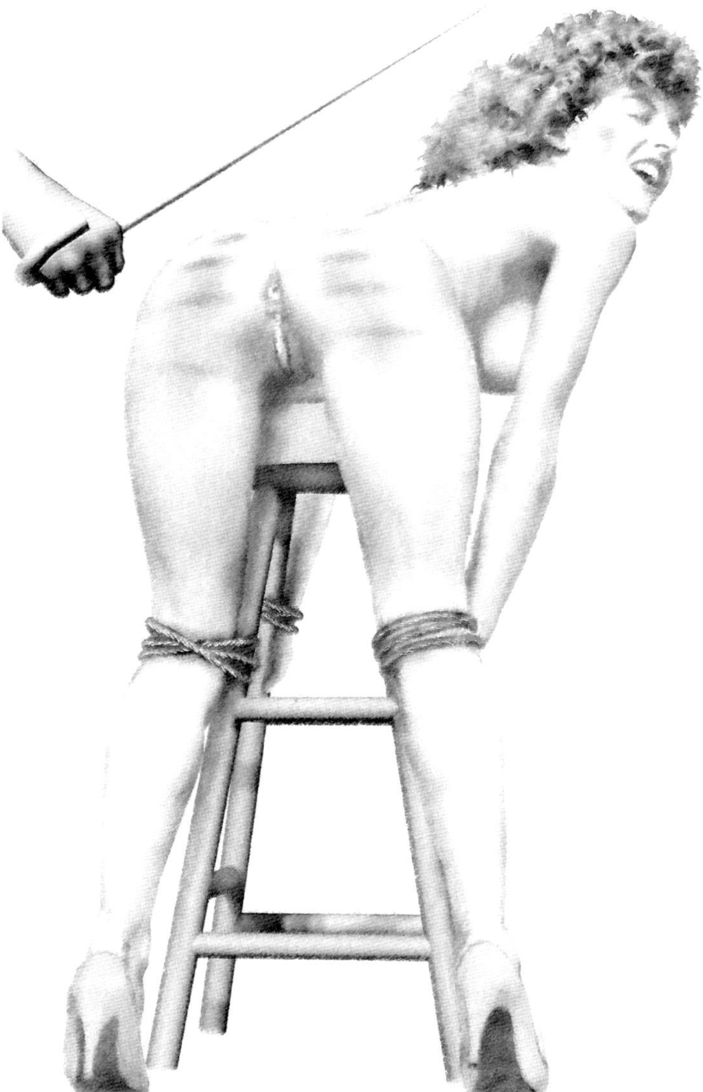

CONTROL YOUR PLEASURE

If I'm using a sex toy to add a little buzz to my excitement, then now is a good time to switch it on. I have a discreet penisator (a vibrator for men in case you didn't know!) that is nice and quiet, which I can leave on at a constant frequency, and draw out the beating for as long as I need, before I climax. It clips nicely onto the end of my erect cock and has a variable controller that I can hold in my free hand, so that I can turn up the juice at just the right moments, and not spoil things by blowing my nuts all over her bare, shivering arse before we're properly finished.

If you don't have such a machine, you can just use your hand, but that makes precise control of the cane more difficult, and besides, I'm a rightie when it comes to pulling my pud as well as beating her bottom and I'd consider it ill-mannered to pause her punishment just to have a wank. On the downside, my technological todger tickler does need to be whipped off before I can shove my log into either of her straining holes, but that's a minor inconvenience, compared to the exquisite control that this wonderful modern device brings to my level of genital excitement.

As for her climax, given the right calibre of female, it should be possible for an expert to beat her right to the edge of her own erotic frenzy. I like to augment this vigorously with my fingers during inspections between stroke sets (deliciously humiliating for her!) and complete the circuit of love after the whipping by mounting her while she still clings tightly to the stool, weeping for mercy and forgiveness.

While my strong hips but against her aching stripes, and my granite piston grinds hard between her squeezing thighs, she can feel her identity slip away in a rapturous tornado of pleasure-pain, and I can finally cement the romantic bond that simultaneous arrival always brings with a special delivery of ounce after ounce of white hot protein floss to decorate her little pink fairground.

And no, it doesn't make the caning hurt less.

But we're getting ahead of ourselves. She hasn't been beaten yet.

BEGINNING THE BEATING

"Now gather your strength, girl. This time, I'm going to make you wet yourself."

That notion always intrigues me a little. It's so poetic to conjure the image of her involuntary urination, forced by the pain and anxiety of my beating her arse. The romance of this is purely symbolic, of course. Readers may disagree, but to me, there's nothing really to be emotionally treasured in mopping up a pool of hot girlswee from the study carpet.

Yet to utter these threats makes her feel so utterly possessed, with her soft, feminine spirit pinched helplessly between the thumb and forefinger of my manly gaze, so we both like to dream that if I whack her extra hard, it will bring about this degrading golden shower, achieve the punishment infinitum, and literally strip away her last vestige of self-control with an orgasmic, bladder-draining cane swipe across her naked bottom.

It thrills me more than a little, I have to admit. But not indoors, darling, there's a good girl.

And so she tenses her body, in a vain attempt to prepare herself for the first stroke, and I start to beat her to my heart's content, "low and slow" as I like to say, savouring every lash and cry as she wriggles and whines under the cane for my inner pulsing pleasure.

It's hard to breathe, sometimes. For both of us.

WHACK! "Take that, girl!"

"Yeeeeeeeeeeeooowwwwwww! One, Sir! Oooh, ow, oooohhhh…… Ahhh…"

She gets sternly lectured between the madness of the whacks:

"Now this is for your own good, young lady" WHACK!

Then harshly scolded, WHACK! "You naughty little minx!"

And even cruelly taunted, WHACK! "Does that hurt your little bare bottom, girl? Ooh, this is the best fun a man can have!"

I then like to begin to show off, calling out the strokes:

"I'm going to put this next one just underneath that last one" WHACK!

"Another one there, right in the same place, I think, don't you?" WHACK!

"Ow!!!!! Yes Sir! Six, Sir!" is the only allowable response to that kind of stomach churning, rhetorical question.

DRAWING OUT THE PUNISHMENT

There are longer pauses between sets while I stroke and slap her bare bum expectantly, finger her fanny, and measure my progress by questioning her:

"Any more smart remarks, girl? Good! I didn't think so."

I punctuate the interrogation with hard taps on the bottom and pussy, using the tip of the cane to poke, stroke, slap and invade, as if I still need to attract and hold her terrified attention.

I also often stop, fold my arms and lean on her bare back to philosophise on the value and pleasure of a sound beating, how wet it is clearly making her, and how hard it is making me, how I can smell the heat of her snatch, and how beneficial it is to her training and character to be whipped to within an inch of insanity by her beloved teacher, prince and master.

"You belong to me, girl. Just you remember that."

Then I may fall wistfully silent only to smack her presented rump with my palm and sigh with relish, as she jumps like a fish wriggling on a hook, "Well, anyway, back to the task in hand."

TO THE VICTOR, THE SPOILS

As I slowly whip her to a quivering jelly, and contemplate her thrashing and debasement out loud, talking myself into adding an additional set or two for good measure, I become so excited, so tense that my pounding hard on will actually jump in time to the beating of my racing heart. And I can always tell by the depth and wobble of her own wails, the wet droplets shining on her inner thighs, and that incredible, provocative, signature scent of her naked tail, that she too is nearing an intoxicating peak of pleasure.

And sure enough, as I deliver the last, stinging lash with my magic wand, timed to perfection, she will cry out louder than ever, suddenly ready to begin her musical chorus of joy as her knees buckle and her kicking legs fall weak. This is the signal for me to throw off my little cockshaker, which by this time has vibrated me close to my own frenzied explosion.

Twisting the twin fibres of torment and joy deep into her hot and bucking snakepit, it doesn't take her trembling, ecstatic anguish long to drain the last of the happy juice out of me in the most pleasurable way imaginable. I have to hold the cane between my teeth and bite down hard as I growl in ejaculatory rage, and she sucks the endless tickling jets from my bone with her straining snatch.

PASSION AND ROMANCE

Sometimes after milking, I just perch there with my hands on her back, patting her scalded hips and leaning forward to kiss her shoulders and neck with such tenderness and love that I never want us to decouple and exist apart.

Otherwise, she sits naked on my lap in my desk chair,

facing me with her thighs supported thoughtfully by my spread knees, to allow her suspended bottom to cool between my open legs and we hug in timeless comfort, each of us enraptured by the other's heated sighs. We sometimes fall asleep like that.

But here I speak of treasured memories, and life has a way of moving on. As I write these fond words, I am a singleton again, finding solace in the pen and keypad in the absence of a special friend to beat.

Sometimes lonely, yes, but never truly alone. Even in these quiet times, with lovers come and gone, my cane and I are never far apart. You see I keep careful custody of that fabulous whipping staff, no matter what the dictates of love and destiny may be.

The cane is a wise thing, a symbol of the power of a man over his woman, of me over my chosen wench, and to me, as it peeps out from behind the study door, it whispers sweetly of adventures yet to come.

Yes, my trusty bamboo friend, there is both comfort and promise in that. There will be someone special and new, and we shall rediscover and explore the miraculous powers of the magic wand together.

You see, even worshipful maids may choose to stay only a while: to bask in my stern adoration before they go their own sweet ways. But I shall always love the cane.

Forever.

WARMING HER BARE PUSSY

As I have already mentioned, long and established patterns of loving discipline routine dictate that when I take ownership of a squaw, it is my usual habit to cane her hard upon her delightful naked and quivering bottom with great passion, vigour and expertise every Sunday evening.

I usually find that this exciting weekly pleasure of mine is enough by itself to keep her pretty behind firmly in line for the next seven days, but this is far too infrequent to slake my potent thirst for female punishment.

In fact, it is one of the most important rules in our house that she should make herself available for a good, sound and satisfying whipping whenever I feel that my stirring cock would be amused by the exertions involved in putting her firmly in her place across my knee for a stern, knickerless whacking.

Therefore, when I am not carefully skinning her hot little tail over my desk with the bamboo, I never tire of slippering her shapely cheeks as an enjoyable means by which to raise the hairs on the back of her neck and stiffen my erection.

I find there's nothing like giving her a good ass whupping to get me in the mood for an ejaculation, whether I intend to simply lather her firm, presented cheeks where she lies, or climb aboard the cheeky minx to pin her down while I shaft her until her feet twitch.

To maximise my enjoyment of this disciplinary diversion, I have this unique reinforced school plimsoll that I use to whack her naked bottom with whenever it tickles my foreplay fancy to beat her backside to a heated, kicking frenzy.

I don't call it spanking though. That doesn't sound sexually humiliating enough for my taste. I prefer to refer to it as the art of "warming her bare pussy."

"Get your knickers off, wench. I'm going to warm that bare pussy today."

That sounds better.

And guess what, readers? It's true! To her immense chagrin, her bare pussy does get decidedly warm when I joyfully go to work, vibrating her pouting tail with my beloved plimsoll. Very warm, and sticky wet. A naughty little fox with a greasy little tail, you might say – and I do - just to make her blush.

Over the years I've lost count of the hours that each of my beloved girls must have spent over my knee in my study taking it hard on the naked arse, having her "bare pussy warmed" as I wallop her to my heart's content. Every man should have a hobby, and whipping the hot bottom cheeks of a submissive maid with a moist and open vulva is satisfying recreation indeed.

If I could bottle that scent I would make a fortune. I think I'd market it under the name: "Spanked Bitch In Heat".

Though it is my custom to live alone with my servant girl, I often think that if there were anyone else out there in the corridor they would enjoy the sounds as I beat her: the dull thumps of the bare pussy warming rhythm, as that tingling rubber pounds against her taut bum, meshed with her coughing gasps of excited but quiet desperation as each burning spank brings her ever closer to the twat-clenching breaking point that I always so diligently seek.

Wop! Uh! … Wop! Uh! … Wop Uh! … Wop! Uh! … Wop! Uh! … Wop Uh…!

Locked together, we form a hot and panting machine of humiliation and punishment.

I know she can hear the fierce, delighted smile on my face as I look fondly down on her reddening behind and deliberately enunciate my intent through gritted teeth, careful not to interrupt the pace, intensity or depth of my whacking tempo:

"We … are … going … to … teach … you … how … to … behave … young … lady … if … I … have … to … warm … your … bare … pussy … for … half … an … hour … by … god … I … swear … I'll … whack … you … until … your … anus … twitches … do … you … hear … me … you … little … minx …?"

And while I punish her, she must just keep to her task of holding her bottom firm and spread for me – "feet up, cheeks apart", as I like to say - knowing that all I want to hear is the breath pushed out of her lungs with each hackle-raising impact, as the heat sinks deep into her bottom, seeking her sensitive, wobbling core.

Wop! Uh! … Wop! Uh! … Wop Uh! … Wop! Uh! … Wop! Uh! … Wop Uh…!

I let her relax long enough to groan when I pause mid whacking to sniff the hot rubber, pat her scalded cheeks and burrow my finger playfully into the sensitive spots that girls have such an abundance of between their open, naked thighs. But more on that amusing little pastime in a moment.

Then, I breathe deeply, mop my brow and clap my hands with glee.

"Phew! My goodness this is making my cock hard! Ready for round two, my bare-bottomed little bitch? Feet up, cheeks apart! Let's warm that pussy good and hard!"

And then we're off again, the bare pussy-warming machine in remorseless motion. With her leg muscles tense as knotted ropes as they desperately strain to keep her feet still for me, the pressure in her quim gradually builds up to an unbearable peak. It's no contest really, between my powerful, accurate whacks to her burning tail, and the helpless, aching and quivering arousal of her snatch.

Wop! Uh! … Wop! Uh! … Wop Uh! … Wop! Uh! … Wop! Uh! … Wop Uh…!

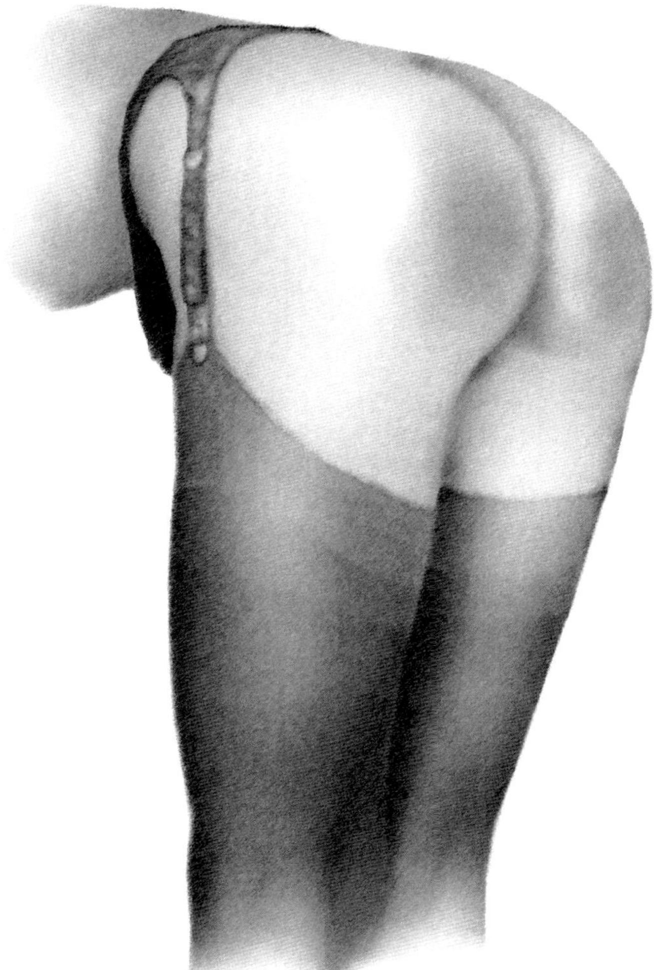

I like to beat her with gusto and tight-lipped satisfaction, slowly grinding away at her pathetic attempts to withhold her shameful sexual secretions and contain the release that is boiling up inside her ready to burst. I feel as though I am delightedly twisting the cork on a bottle of champagne whilst vigorously shaking it: forcing her to pop, but at an excruciating pace that I alone control.

Until eventually she loses her grip on everything:

Wop! Aaah! Wop! Aaaaaah! Wop! Yeeeeeoooooww oooohhh! Ooooohhhh!

"Yeuck! Ha! You messy little cow! Look at all that sticky goo! What a disgrace. Where's your self control, girl? What a racket!"

I can rest my arm now, and wiggle my fingers playfully in the warm pink softness of her split, while she kicks and wails of her own accord, both of us feeling that bare pussy twitching inside as well as out. How degrading to have her naked bottom whacked and walloped until she cries out in the throes of uncontrolled wet and hot, erotic spasm! And all for my own sexual amusement.

I laugh at her, push a celebratory cigar up her bottom and shake my head while she hangs hers in broken and exhausted shame. As I wipe her own sticky juices from my trembling hand onto her scalded bum, I know in my bones that victory is complete, and completely mine, and so is she. All that remains is to decide where to leave my own white-hot, slimy calling card, and how long to make her wear it before I wash her down.

In the bedroom, I prefer a slightly different routine. First thing in the morning, or perhaps last thing at night, she must wait for me by the bed, dressed in a negligee, or t-shirt, socks and flimsy, straining panties, while I fetch my stout wooden ruler: the dreaded "Pussy Whacker".

I don't even need to speak, just sit down on the bed, pat my waiting lap and wait for her to assume the punishment position yet again: knickers down, feet up, cheeks apart, bare pussy ready for warming.

That ruler really scorches and it makes a fantastic sound when I whack it across her naked bottom. That and the smell of clean bed linen framing the scent of her wet musk makes me come quite quickly from bedroom spankings, especially in the morning when I'm usually pitching a tent before I even wake up.

I need quite a lot of orgasms – about once a day, every day does me just fine, though I have to say that when I was a teenager, I felt short changed if I didn't spray away some happiness three times every twenty-four hours. Too much testosterone, I guess.

Even my current daily squirt however adds up to too much punishment for even the fittest bottom. Of course I love to blow my nuts the most either during or after giving my bitch a good walloping. As master to my girl, it's an enjoyable aspect of my job, which I do to the best of my considerable ability.

But when her tail is too sore for recreational beating, she must make her hindquarters available in a suitable mounting posture, so that I may relieve my powerful needs in a more conventional fashion: riding my little pony bareback round the bed, as we like to say in my home.

As an alternative to the nocturnal gymkhana, I find I can achieve a very satisfying release by taking her across my knee and instead of delivering a spanking, practise the traditional Japanese art of jeni tala goni, where precise pressures are applied with the fingertips to the nerve centres of the female pudendum to create by turns either unbearable pain or ecstatic pleasure.

A woman oscillating moment by moment between clit tickling excitement and fanny straining torture, wriggles and screams in a most pleasing and unique fashion, in one instant unable to escape my strong fingers, and in the next, burrowing her lettuce down upon them. Girls say that it engenders an intolerable burning of anxiety, distress, aching lust and frustration that sets their whole insides aflame with sexual torture.

You've got to love those Japanese. They really know how to treat their women. Legend has it that one of the Shoguns used to organise feasts where ten girls would be tied naked over special frames in the centre of the hall, bottoms high in the air. A jeni tala goni exponent would sit between the bare and tethered thighs of each female and begin to apply a long series of hellish pinches and agonising tweaks to her helpless, pouting labial hotspots throughout the evening.

The genital torment of each girl would be coordinated with all the others so that the chorus of groans, sighs, shrieks and sobs from the poor maids would fill the air with a carefully choreographed symphony of tormented ecstasy as the girls were drilled through an endless succession of what I like to think of as female agonisms: the climaxes achieved by women through the controlled application of pain.

This sado-erotic recital was a special entertainment for samurai who had just returned victorious from battle, and the girls subjected to this twat-snapping ordeal were considered to be receiving a great honour. Younger and less prestigious geisha girls would nurse the erections of the warriors while they ate, drank and listened to the suffering songs of the bound and naked wenches, tending to their masters' ejaculations with skill and enthusiasm, hoping one day to earn an honoured place upon the jeni tala goni frames.

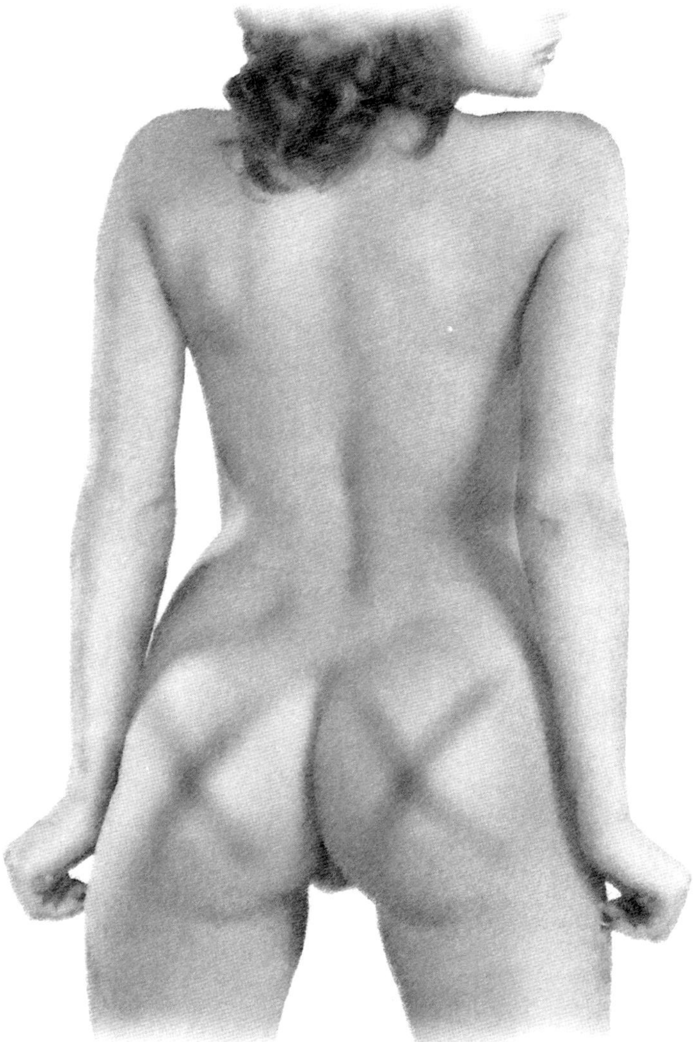

I've often thought that each expert would have to spend long hours practising with his female instrument, so that he could make her produce the exact desired sounds at the right time. Otherwise the whole thing would sound a bit discordant, but the men probably would have enjoyed it nonetheless.

It's a lovely story though.

Anyway mythology aside, there are some advanced jeni tala goni techniques – called the floating world tormentations – that will take her beyond her senses, causing her to faint as she peaks in breathless, ecstatic agony, but these are not for the beginner, being very difficult to apply correctly even under ideal conditions, let alone to the bucking, slippery hindquarters of a quivering girl, and even very strong females will need to be tied and given something stout to bite on while they endure this.

But the basic pinch and stretch combinations, together with the highly amusing clitoral excruciations are quite easy to master with just a basic understanding of female genital anatomy, and the threat of ever more severe techniques and harder pinching pressures should ensure that she keeps herself in place, with thighs spread while you patiently explore her full vocal range, and gradually extend her struggling limits of endurance.

An unnaturally resilient girl can be tormented in this way for over an hour, but some self-control on my part is required for such lengthy experimentation upon a female's private parts while her thigh and buttock muscles clench and release in time to her desperate gasps and groans. I find that as she squeals and mewls her way to her own spectacularly watery explosion, it becomes inevitable that my happy sacks will empty almost of their own accord, unless I try to think of something else every five or ten minutes.

No, if she is to enjoy the benefits of prolonged labial

agony, then it is incumbent upon me to master the considerable pressure that builds up in my own aching balls during the breathless eternities of her humiliating distress.

It's a good exercise in self-control for me as well as her, even if we do both have to surrender in the end: she to the unbearable haze of intimate pain, me to the hot tingly bolts of pleasure that managing her wriggling perspiration excites within my loins.

That said, it is a most agreeable hobby, and well worth the two to three hours of practise that I make sure to put in every week. There are even special doughnut shaped cushions that you can buy from the chemist that make it possible for her to sit down in relative comfort during the difficult 24 hours that follow a prolonged session of jeni tala goni manipulations.

I mention all this because it is my habit to only allow her to refer to her sexual releases as actual "orgasms", when they occur during what we touchingly call our "proper fucks".

Any climactic catharsis that I am able to wring out of her by means of punishment or recreational punishment of her genitals or anus is not worthy of the same name, no matter how mind blowing and intense it may feel to her shattered dignity.

No, she must be brought to understand that when I talk about warming her bare pussy, that is my way of saying that I intend to slipper or torment her to a climax, but I will never refer to any vaginal explosion that she experiences over my knee as "climactic". To me it is just her "bare pussy twitching".

Sometimes I refer to her heated sex emissions as "squirts" or "dribbles" and to "wringing out her fanny like a sopping flannel", but to me, a whipping squaw is too lowly to properly come during a beating, and certainly should never be credited with an “ejaculation” no matter how far and how proudly her vaginal fountain erupts under the plimsoll.

An orgasm is something that I experience and enjoy while I am giving her bare pussy a good hard warming, but as the naughty little wench pressed firmly down under my strong thumb, she is to be considered beneath such refined pleasures.

“Never forget, little minx,” I like to say as I thrash the living daylights out of her naked behind or torment her privates to an agonising frenzy, “that I can wallop you until your fanny squirts or tweak your pussy until you piss yourself, whenever and wherever I please, simply because I am better than you.

“That’s why I enjoy warming your bare pussy until you squeal. Because you’re just a pathetic little mouse. Now shut up while I beat your bottom just for fun. I’m going to whack you until your naked pussy twitches then tie a knot in your clit with my fingers, and there’s nothing you can say or do about it.

“Cheeks apart, feet up, girl!”

“Let’s warm that bare pussy: good and hard!”

HOW TO SPANK A WOMAN: PART 1

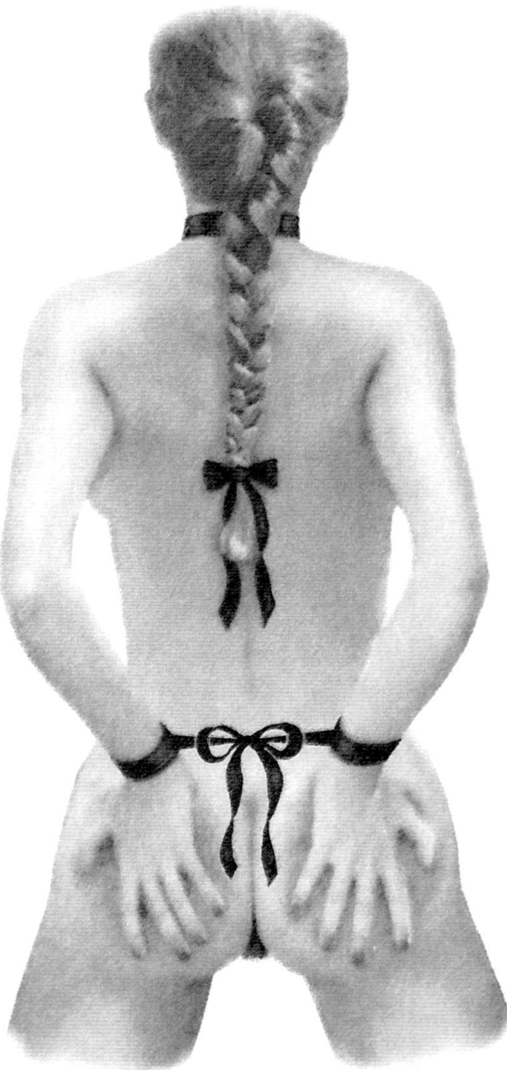

THE FEMALE BOTTOM DESERVES A PROPER SPANKING

Nature provided the female of our species with her uniquely attractive hindquarters so that the twin threads of spanking and sex can be woven together into whatever wonderful tapestry her man desires.

It's no coincidence after all, that having thrashed her naked cheeks until they positively glow, the spanking wench is both totally subdued, and perfectly presented in a fine mounting posture. My blacksmith tells me that hot iron needs quenching in the bucket until the water boils, and when I stand rigid over the spanked and trembling bottom of a freshly disciplined girl, I have no choice but to follow his code.

Conversely, as a cultured as well as a superior gentleman, I would also consider it very negligent to give my chosen maid a pussyful of the royal granite, without first warming her lovely bottom until she squeals. This is a delightful reminder to her that love her though he does, there is by natural law, significant difference in the status between a brave and his squaw.

It also conforms to the spirit of that famous English adage: that one should always warm the pot, to ensure the perfect cup of tea.

In conclusion, I consider punishing the female bottom not only to be a man's duty, but also to constitute one of his life's greatest pleasures. As such, like all classic pastimes, it should be enjoyed with the proper skill and attention to detail.

Now, fascinated as I am by the art of disciplining the naked tails of naughty girls, I have a large archive of wonderful of spanking materials including a huge library of images and movies carefully selected from the cornucopia of such delights that pepper the internet.

Really authentic footage of fellow experts is hard to come by though. In many of these illustrative guides to the punitive tuition of the female posterior, I am often shocked by the poor quality of the whippings administered to the beautiful and submissively offered behinds on display.

Some of the treatment I see meted out to exotically beautiful women with the most delicious bottoms is really quite shoddy and amounts to nothing less than a litany of spanking crimes. It is an absolutely shocking waste of those finely presented and delectable tails.

When a girl bares her behind over your bed, desk or knee, it is your sacred duty to administer those delightful whacks with loving care, and that means being in full and proper control of your own punishment technique, as well as her rear, from first bend to final squeal.

With this most basic premise in mind, I intend in a series of short articles to outline some of the worst and most common lapses in punishment etiquette that I have seen, together with a guide to easy steps that may be taken by any male to correct those deficiencies in his own spanking method.

In Part 2 I intend to address the fundamental aspects of proper bottom smacking.

HOW TO SPANK A WOMAN: PART 2

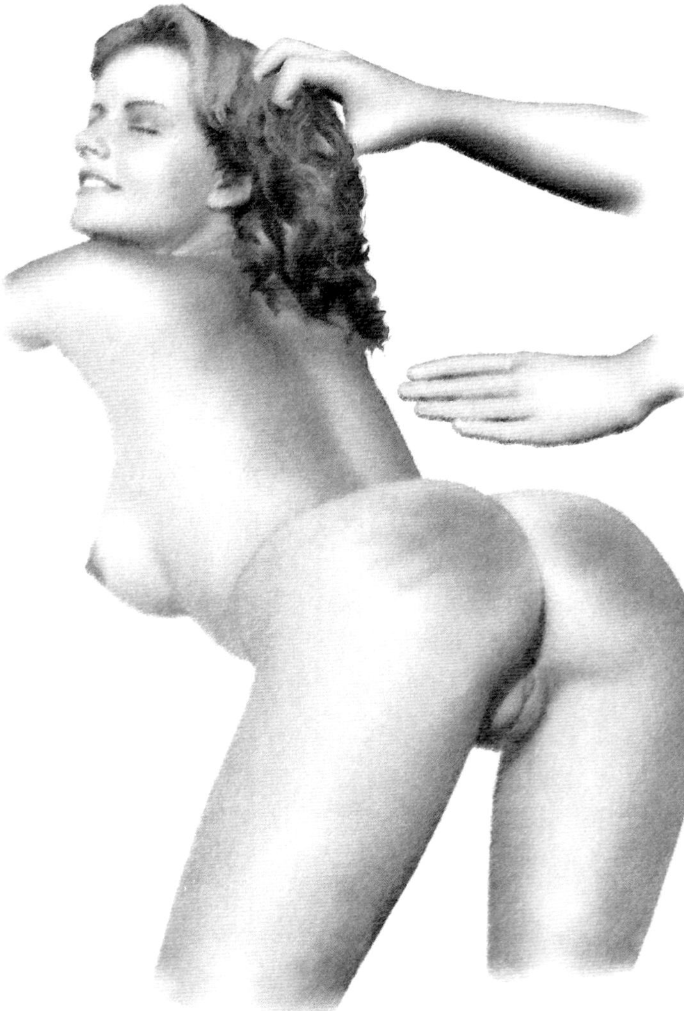

PROPER SMACKING

Following on from my introduction, I intend to give detailed instructions on how to apply correct spanks to your wench's comely tail. Following the simple guidelines presented here, it will be perfectly possible for any considerate gentleman to wallop the hindquarters of his servant girl or student to his perfect satisfaction. Moreover, though her ears may pop and her privates twitch, his unlucky maid should endure no more lasting an injury than a temporary inability to sit, and a profound reluctance to disobey in the future.

The worst crime a spanker can commit is commonly called "punching" a girl's bottom. The sorry fact is that these posterior pugilists believe that they are spanking their charge, when in fact they are just beating up her back end.

What is "punching"? Simply put, it is when the spanker thumps the heel of his palm into his girl's bottom. The dull sound of a punch is unmistakable as it drives unpleasantly into her buttocks, bruising muscles deeply and quite unnecessarily. Everyone who begins to spank his girl regularly will occasionally "punch" her bottom by accident every once in a black and blue moon, but to do so as a matter of habit is ignorance and just sheer brutality.

Anyone who cares even a little about the health and happiness of his lady friend should learn how to smack her behind properly and humanely before taking her over his knee for a prolonged session of chastisement. Take a minute to consider the following advice and then compare it to your own technique:

The correct slap or bottom smack is delivered with the hand relaxed, fingers together, curled slightly to meet and match the curve of the bottom cheek upon impact. Watch how a seasoned spanker always measures his palm against her buttock before delivering his smack. Whether he knows it or not, he is measuring the shape of his target area with his hand so that he gets his contact slap precisely right and full, whether he is spanking on the round of the buttock, thigh, undercurve or pussy (ouch!)

Keeping all tension out of the fingers but the wrist straight, so that the hand is poised but heavy, the full power of impact is applied with the base of the fingers just above and below where they join the palm. The fingertips and the rest of the palm will follow automatically and instantaneously, and a loud, resonant SLAP! should echo pleasantly around the room. There is no need to follow through – the shock wave will penetrate right from anus to pussy from a satisfying and proper contact – but the palm can be dragged slightly if a longer burn is required.

What is the burn? A good hard smack will hurt her in two ways: these are traditionally known as the "sting" and the "burn". The sharper "sting" is felt immediately on impact, and should literally raise the hairs on the back of her neck. Most girls will make an involuntary "Ahh!" sound at this sharp pain, even if it is their habit or intention to say "Ow!" or "Oooh!" while being walloped. Listen carefully for this note or alternatively a sharp inhalation of air, and you can be sure you are generating a good, smart sting.

The lovely "burn" follows the sting and creeps deeper into the skin. It is a much hotter and more prolonged pain that dies away gradually. It is this sensation that builds during a spanking and makes her wriggle and kick her legs so delightfully. An accomplished spanker will land each succeeding smack before the scalding pain of the last one has faded way, and in so doing gradually build up an unbearable furnace of heat in the poor girl's reddening tush.

Rather than the somewhat coarse practice of fast spanking

(which makes the ungentlemanly act of punching more likely) the expert learns to lengthen the burn by dragging the palm slightly as mentioned above, at the very moment of impact. A proper drag is a very slight movement across the bottom – less than a quarter inch – that intensifies and prolongs the cheek burn. It takes practice, but adepts will appreciate that this makes leisurely stroke selection, and even a pat or two, possible before the next whack is due.

A slow spanker is a spanker in control, and such patient technique allows more effective scolding and intimate exploration between smacks and gives a greater opportunity generally to savour the sights, sounds and scents of a woman enduring a difficult punishment.

The crowning glory of this kind of proper spanking technique is that a seasoned bottom, spanked regularly, can be given fifty to a hundred smacks at a sitting, reducing the girl to a trembling jelly of bare-bottomed submission to your will, while inflicting no more than a very red rear, and leaving you with a rather numb and tingly palm, but no significant bruising to either of you.

In fact, a half century of proper, loving smacks should see her quite capable of assuming the position again after twenty-four hours, should it be your pleasure to beat her again the next day. Indeed, I prefer that my girl should receive this kind of attention three or four nights in the week, with perhaps a hundred smacks delivered in a double sitting at the weekend on the rare occasions she is not caned on a Sunday evening.

A sedate and measured spanking can also be administered at a pace that suits you. There's no need for you to be panting and gasping in an undignified manner – leave that to her, while you mercilessly demand that she count her way to as high a number as you choose, making the last hackle-raising wallop as unbearable as the first.

Additionally, proper smacks as described above, are just as effective on tensed buttocks, tight buns or soft, ample curves as they are on hips, thighs, hamstrings or pussies. Personally, I prefer my girl to present with thighs apart, secrets exposed and feet off the floor to keep her bottom taut. This provides a gratifying resistance to hard slaps, but keeps everything submissively displayed for my enjoyment while her feet are free to twitch in time to her gasps and squeaks.

This is just my own inclination. I know gentlemen who prefer to punish clenched, rigid buttocks atop straight legs and others who love to watch the rippling of submissively relaxed cheeks under their palms. A correct smacking technique will work perfectly well upon any of the above presentations.

In Part 3 I intend to address the wriggly issue of allowing a girl over your knee to struggle pleasantly, without escaping, slipping out of position, or even slightly interfering with even the most unbearable spanking.

HOW TO SPANK A WOMAN: PART 3

HOLDING HER DOWN

With the best will in the world, some girls are twitchy, flighty, and just plain awkward to beat once their knickers are down. Of course, witnessing her struggle to contain the fire you are lighting across her bare cheeks is one of the warmest joys of administering a prolonged arse-whipping. However her writhing should be restricted by training and restraint to remain a source of pleasing entertainment, and should never be allowed to develop into a frustrating impediment to the delivery of her just desserts.

With the methods I shall outline below, even the wriggliest wench can be subdued in a dignified fashion while she receives her whacks, and howls to your heart's content.

METHOD 1: HEAD DOWN, GIRL!

This is a surprisingly simple suggestion but often effective. With the girl in position over your knee, put your hand firmly against the back of her head and instruct her "Head down!" This can have an almost magically subduing effect on even the most rebellious squaw. Unfortunately, her head may reflexively jerk up after extra hard smacks on the bottom (in fact, it might be your habit to actually encourage occasional glances upwards if you use mirrors to enhance her degradation as I prefer to do). Therefore I recommend that you periodically check her head position and readjust it when necessary. Don't forget the firm verbal command; "Down, girl."

METHOD 2: LOOK, NO HANDS!

One of the most annoying and frustrating things to see, is a girl repeatedly reaching back to protect her naked bottom with one or both hands, or even worse, restrain the arm of the man trying to whack some sense into her.

This shows a lack of authority on the part of the spanker. Now I know that some girls will say that they can't help but try to protect themselves when a spanking is hurting and some men do like their female to physically demonstrate a profound reluctance to be punished, but I firmly believe that neither of these excuses properly pardon this blatant disregard for basic spanking etiquette, which demands that she must be taught to submit to your dominant pleasure, especially when she is suffering considerable distress.

Though the female reluctance to fully surrender may be both desirable and involuntary, the defensive use of the hands is certainly neither. She can mount an equally appealing and far less intrusive protest by beating her fists against the floor (or cushions if the pair of you are interlocked on the sofa). She can also be encouraged to verbally protest and even beg you to stop. This can be most exciting.

If she shows a clear need to grip something tightly, try the following: I sometimes allow a girl over my lap to hold both ends of a short rope or tea towel, wrap one end around each of her hands and then wring it this way and that as I wallop her. In this way she can magnify my arousal by vigorously demonstrating acute discomfort without interfering even slightly with my scorching attention to her bottom.

For girls who are desperate to hug something during a beating, a large cushion or teddy bear that they can clutch to their chests or faces will do. She may also request something to bite on, and a clean cloth or a pair of her knickers will suffice, or for something with a little more steel, use a clean piece of wood like a pencil. The handle of a wooden spoon is ideal for this, and is sure to be found in the secret drawer of every spanking enthusiast.

Alternatively, she can be commanded to keep her hands somewhere out of the way, say with her arms folded behind her back. She can even fold her hands behind her head or be made to hold them out straight in front of her. The advantage of this latter possibility is that in the otk position in a freestanding chair, it keeps her back nicely arched and lifts her bottom at the same time. She may have to keep her feet on the floor though to prevent overbalancing.

Enforced hand positions are good discipline and more than a little cute, but in whatever pose she is ordered to maintain them, command that she concentrate on keeping them tense from shoulders to fingertips for the duration of her thrashing. This will prevent the unwanted blocking urges from re-emerging during stressful punishment.

Of course, if your girl has developed deeply ingrained unruly habits, a period of readjustment and training may be necessary. It is my experience that a simple sliding scale of punishment need only be applied once or twice to effect a complete re-education of a girl who claims that she can't stop herself from fighting you off.

Begin her usual spanking with the implement you customarily use to discipline her, but keep at least two additional implements, each harsher than the last within easy reach. Once you have her bare-bottomed over your knee, explain to her what is going to happen: that each time she reaches back towards her rear, the spanking will stop, and you will start again – from the beginning – with a sharper instrument.

For example, if you traditionally smack her bottom with your bare hand, a good, stiff, wooden ruler is a suitable choice for turning up the heat on her toasting buns. If she doesn't get that message clearly, then leave a really scorching impression on both her psyche and her naked behind with a flat backed hairbrush.

This nearly always works and gives an incomparable sensation of accomplishment. "I think you've learned your lesson, young lady," is the way I like to express my sense of conquest before mounting her to cement my victory.

With these simple techniques it should never be necessary to tie a girl's hands, but this is always an option for those who enjoy these extra touches of domination and control. Interestingly, some girls who swear blind that they can't help struggling like fish in a sand pit when they're having their naked bottoms spanked, will lie meekly in place when their hands are tied while you tan the living daylights out of their bare, quivering tails. Ah, the mystery that is woman.

Tying the wrists in front or behind her back will completely frustrate her desire to interfere with your palm. To secure wrists easily and gently but effectively, use a small rope or strong ribbon, and capture one wrist in a loose(ish) over and under loop (think of starting to tie your shoelaces) and then pin the other wrist to the first with another identical loop. This time, finish off the bow (think shoelaces again) and she will be secured no matter how hard she pulls, release being a simple matter of a gentle tug of one of the free ends.

METHOD 3: KICKING THE KICKING HABIT.

Nearly every man likes a girl to kick at least a little while he spanks her. Those little spasms and twitches in time to the gasps, squeaks and yelps are a visual confirmation that you are doing your job as a male. They also reveal and conceal the pussy and anus by turns, and get the fresh scents of girl-sweat and she-musk into the air while her bucking hips rub electrically against your unavoidably rigid manhood.

What is not so wonderful, is when her foot flies up, heel first into the back of your hand as you withdraw it from her bum, or worse, jerks up between your fingers and her naked cheeks as you try to deliver a real stinger of a slap. If she has shoes on, you can break or dislocate a finger in this way. Not a good way to loose your spanking hand for six weeks.

Now of course the legs can be trained in the same way as the arms: making sure that her feet don't fly up too high is as easy as persuading her to keep her hands to herself. But for men who prefer a more physical approach to the subjugation of their girls, why not try using your own legs to restrain hers?

Let's suppose that you are right handed. Put her between your legs as you sit on the edge of your spanking chair, and have her bend over your left knee. With her arms folded, elbows on the floor, her bottom and pussy are upturned right in front of you when she parts her thighs. This affords a much better view of her privates than the traditional over-both-knees position and makes it easier to check her state of arousal periodically whether you prefer to do this by taste, touch, sight or scent. You can also get a gravity assist and use downward smacks for greater sting and deeper burn. Access to her very sensitive undercurves is much easier as well from here. Remember to spank them hard.

Now that you have her naked and upturned ass in position, you can use your right leg to pin hers. Decide whether you prefer to lock both her legs to immobilise them completely while she wriggles in distress, or just grip the left one, using your right knee to separate her thighs as wide as you require. Full separation of the thighs or “wishboning” can be both humiliation and torment for a woman, depending upon how flexible her hips are, and it certainly makes spanking between the buttocks much easier (see below for a brief discussion of this practice).

If you decide just to pin her left leg, her free right leg can thrash around madly to flag her unbearable distress, but will be unlikely to interfere with the punishment, as you apply spanks enthusiastically from your comfortable position, above and to her left.

Lean heavily on the small of her back with your left hand, and she will know she’s not going anywhere until you’ve finished with her. Squaws who enjoy the sensations of being fully controlled will be trapped firmly in spanking heaven.

Although it is gloriously displayed and wide open to invading fingers, it’s not easy to spank the pussy from this position so I generally tend to punctuate the scolding by just tapping her quim threateningly or pinching it if I want her to make a wide variety of different squeaks. It is very easy to deliver some more unusual spanks though, notably to the inside left of her buttock cleft. Wishbone her cheeks wide with your leg so that you can land the smack with the little finger edge of your hand as close to her anus as possible. To do the other side, turn her round, so that she’s bending over your right knee. You’ll have to apply the slap upside down, but with practice you'll be able to work up an all over glow right down between her cheeks on both sides.

In my final instalment, I intend to give additional tips to men who wish to generalise these methods and control their girls while caning them.

HOW TO SPANK A WOMAN: PART 4

CANING WITH CONFIDENCE

A final note here on the use of the cane. Although up to now, this treatise has focussed on the fine art of handspanking, I want to spend some time in consideration of the bamboo craft. I feel this to be important, since the most common problem reported to me by men who have enjoyed subjecting their wenches to the severe caning protocols described in an earlier chapter, concerns the issue of control of the squealing girl under punishment.

This discussion properly belongs here, as it follows on naturally from Part 3 of this series, which dealt comprehensively with the logistics by which a man can safely fix a female firmly over his knee while he wallops her naked rear end to his heart's content and complete satisfaction, and uses many of the same binding and restraint techniques.

Now, laying precise whacks with a cane across the bare cheeks of women bending seductively over whipping stools or desks, or simply touching their toes, means that the girls are free to jump to their feet and hop around as the heat of each hard stroke begins to bite. If you enjoy this athletic response to laying on the rod, then fine, but don't fall prey to the myth propagated by these unruly girls that it hurts so much they have no choice but to react in this way.

I like to be in full control of my girl's bottom while I'm caning her, and keeping her in place while I leisurely break her is even more important during a formal caning. If I want to watch her skip from foot to foot and rub her naked cheeks in mid whipping then I give her permission so to do, usually about half way through. This way I never lose charge of her, but still get to enjoy the frisson of quietly ordering her back into position as she reluctantly wiggles her stripes back over the stool in front of me.

For men having trouble with leaping ladies I would recommend the following.

She almost certainly needs some kind of release when she's being whacked with the cane, so first of all, make sure she knows how to cry out properly. A long, loud "ooooowww!" noise full and rounded – a proper shout lasting for a second or two is undignified for her and deeply satisfying for you, believe me.

Inhibited girls may find it hard to let go and howl in this way, so initially you may want to experiment with the binding techniques outlined below first. Tied down to the stool and unable to spring up, she may find that she has no option but to cry out while you beat her, and through this will discover the freedom to yell at the top of her lungs and the discipline within to stay put when, after a few sessions, you decide to stop securing her in place.

The "bit between her teeth" technique and the "something to grip" solutions described in Part 3 of this spanking etiquette series are also relevant here and are applied in exactly the same way. Caners who use a proper stool with a crossbeam may instruct her to grip the spar with both hands. Reflexively clenching her fists around this when each stroke lands will prevent her lifting her hips from the seat. Effectively she holds herself down in a semi-involuntary fashion, which I find quite amusing.

Once a girl is trained to grip a spar right the way through a sound thrashing, she can progress to free standing bends while gripping her own ankles, if that is her master's pleasure. Let her bend her knees one at a time after each whack to release leg tension. I find it very arousing to stand back and watch while she does this. Quick repetitions of this desperate action result in what is touchingly called the "whipping wiggle" and every connoisseur of the cane should witness this at least once in his life, if not once a week!

Alternatively, use a gravity assist to hold her in place: she must kneel on a low table or stool, or the arm of a chair, and place both hands palm-flat on the floor, leaving her ass high in the air. For such a gravity trap to work effectively, her head must be lower than her knees. Make her fold her arms and rest on her elbows to achieve this if necessary.

Not only does this pose make leaping up impossible for her, it also affords an incomparable view of her privates and allows for a most attractive arching of the spine during punishment. Post-punitive copulation was never made so alluring or easy.

As I mentioned above, you can also prevent bounding with binding. Use the simple over-under loop knots and bows described in part 3 in the following ways:

Free standing girls should simply have their wrists fastened to their ankles, but females presenting over stools should have their wrists lashed to the spars or legs of the furniture. Alternatively, loop a thicker rope or long belt under the seat and over the small of her back.

As for binding a girl's legs to a whipping stool, this is a matter of visual preference. If you enjoy a good display of kicking and twitching, leave her legs free. To observe her anus and pussy as they pout in helpless desperation, fix her legs with the thighs held wide.

When tying her legs to separate her bottom cheeks, it is tempting to strap the thighs apart above the knee, and I agree that this allows for a safe and immensely pleasurable display as she thrashes her lower legs up and down during her beating, but there is a somewhat more elegant solution that you might like to try.

Consider tying her ankles to the legs of the stool at a height that keeps her knees bent at around than ninety degrees (that's a right angle or "square corner"). This pushes her knees forward on either side of the stool, separates her bottom cheeks and presents her pussy open and proud behind her. Finish off the bondage by keeping her strapped down to the seat of the stool with a belt as described above, to keep her back nicely arched.

You can then cane her to your heart's content. Every time she wriggles, her sex will push energetically towards you, in a most provocative way, encouraging you to lay on each stroke with excited vigour. When beating girls on the lawn, females that are prone to do so can be allowed to urinate to express their powerless distress. When a girl is tied thus, with her bottom thrust out, the wee wee comes out pony fashion behind her in a short, hygienic arc away from the legs of the stool.

Though this can be an extremely gratifying result, indicative of a fine job done with proper enthusiasm, it is not my habit to normally allow this, but I do not seriously object to it. As an occasional spectacle, it can make a rather rewarding outcome to a sound thrashing, but make sure that you rinse ornamental grass with plenty of fresh tap water afterwards. Whether canine or human, urine is prone to leave a nasty brown burn if left untreated on the turf that can seriously ruin the croquet.

And with this piece of sound advice from my groundsman, I come to the end of this fascinating discussion on the finer points of wench whacking. Remember, spank them long, spank them hard, but for goodness sake, spank them properly.

WHIPPING HER ARSE INTO SHAPE: PART 1

A GUIDE TO BEATING YOUR GIRL'S BOTTOM FOR YOUR FUN AND HER FITNESS

It is with some satisfaction that I like to point out that my years as a strict trainer to pert-bottomed young women have kept me in good physical shape. Now a man in my early forties, the fact that I am not ashamed to get my tits out in my IC (Informed Consent.co.uk) profile photo, should prove that the corporal punishment regime I am about to describe will help to tone and preserve your own physique, as well as her shapely buns.

How have I been able to keep that tummy in trim these long years? Simply put, a life spent comprehensively dominating submissive wenches is physically as well as sexually demanding. This is because the total conquest of a female requires that she frequently be coerced into performing strenuous tasks of quite unnecessary physical exercise solely for the purposes of my enjoyment.

Of course, with an obedient and energetic squaw, ordering her to action can be quite a leisurely pursuit. Taunting her naked body while she pointlessly and loyally toils away at some small lifting routine or posture drill, will often stiffen me very pleasantly between the legs as I recline in my garden chair to sip my drink, watch her bare body shiver with effort, listen to her gasps and grunts of exertion, and scent the heady aroma of fresh girlsweat on the summer breeze.

Of course, after a half hour or so of this gentle teasing of my libido, my excited mood will require more direct pleasuring in the manner of my choosing. For example, twenty minutes on all-fours in front of me may be a delightful way for her to rest her aching muscles, while I seek deep relief between her hot and musky thighs.

Alternatively, a similar period spent on her knees, craning her neck as she tongues her way around my pulsing rod, while I leaf through a back issue of "Janus" and conduct the proceedings ("higher, girl,... oooh! Slower, damn you! Mmmm...") can really ice the cake of her already leg trembling exhaustion, and make a mess of her hair, bottom or whatever other part of her anatomy I use as a handy receptacle for my scalding essence.

Now keeping me thusly entertained and amused by running bare-arsed back and forth, is a good basis for maintaining female health and strength, but I am famous for my deeply imaginative and determined lust for the physical education of my girls. I like nothing better than to muck in when it comes to keeping more lazy wenches fit and active, and I use the extra spurt of sexual energy I derive from their ordeals to spur my own muscular efforts as I chastise them, and thereby keep myself in a healthy and robust condition.

Having developed this pastime to the level of considerable expertise, I intend to lay down the basics here, for any superior male, who wishes to begin introducing his reluctant girl to the healthy rigours of punishment exercise.

I apologise in advance to dominant men who may find some of the instructions I give here to be rather too precise for their liking. This work is not intended to be in any way prescriptive, but is simply a reflection of the very strict way in which I prefer to train the bitch under my whip.

Dominant men should feel free to regard these detailed notes as guidelines only, and anyone thusly angered by my very thorough approach should vent his frustrations by punishing his squealing girl severely in the manner that pleases him most.

As a general rule, I find it is only good practice to blame my squaw for anything that I find distressing or annoying, because this provides a simple and extremely satisfying avenue by which to discharge such pent up negativity: strip her bare and thrash the living daylights out of her. I always feel better after that, and I'm sure you do too.

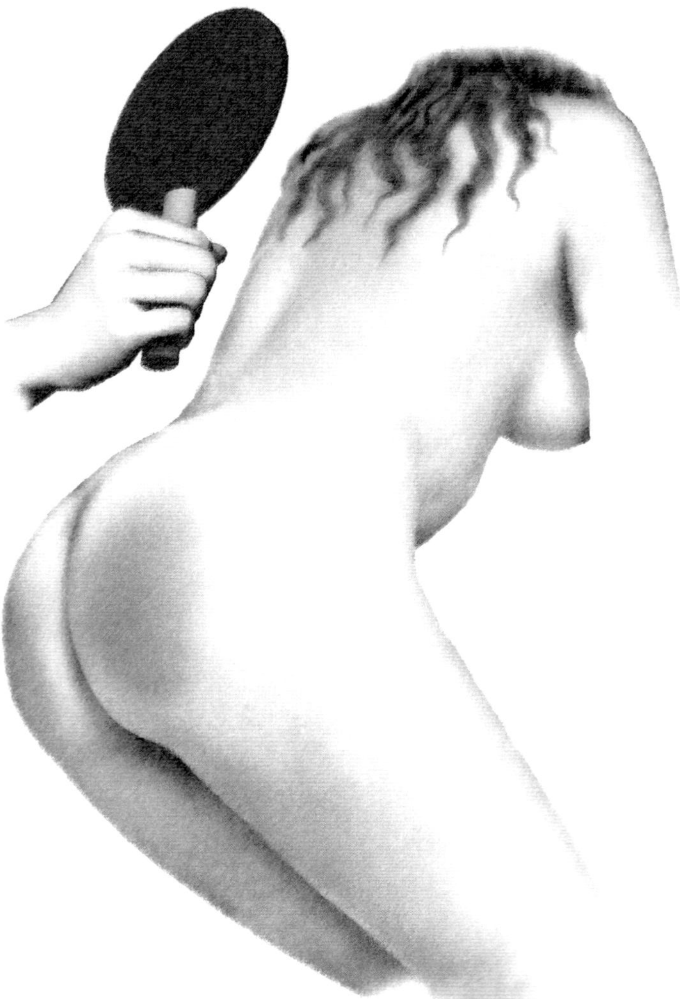

WHERE TO EXERCISE HER

Obviously, if a gentleman is to train a filly naked and whip her constantly during the proceedings, some measure of privacy is essential in today's judgemental world. A large room with furniture that can be easily removed and replaced with basic or improvised gym equipment is the absolute minimum requirement, though I have been lucky enough to train a fit young lady who owned a large, isolated and totally secluded garden.

There she discovered that outdoor training has a quite unique thrill of its own. The sensations of cold grass under her bare feet and bottom, and cool breezes exploring her aroused privates added more than a frisson of humiliation and excitement to the experience of being rigorously put through her paces by her sadistic and very imaginative, grinning master.

For those men not fortunate enough to be able to enjoy working their wenches al fresco, a more formal and educational ambience for indoor training can be achieved by exercising her on bare floorboards. Provided that splinters can be safely avoided, making her run, jump and posture naked on uncarpeted floors makes her feel far more vulnerable and twitchy, and it beautifully enhances the acoustics of the frequent bottom beatings, making the sounds of both whacks and squeals simultaneously more resonant and sharper.

A carpet obviously makes for a softer landing should your charge accidentally upend, bare arse over naked tits, while you orchestrate her trials, but the only indoor surface one should positively avoid in my experience is a dangerous one covered by unglued carpet tiles or a slippery rug. Exercise mats, if they are used, should be of the grippy materials one sees in good yoga and aerobics classes. The session should be made as painful as she can possibly stand, but should not be in any way injurious to her.

WHAT TO BEAT HER WITH

Unlike a formal spanking or caning, where a suitable choice of implement is usually made beforehand, during a PT (punishment training) session many shorter whackings are administered during or between exercises, either to encourage effort or to punish poor performance. In fact, as you read this manual, you will discover that PT really is an amazing spankfest. This means that as a matter of style and sophistication, a wider choice of beating tools must be made easily accessible from the start.

I have found it is possible to derive an immense amount of fun from exploring an exciting variety of slap sticks during a PT scenario, so I will outline a selection of what I consider to be the best ones, but this list is by no means exhaustive and every magician has his own favourite magic wand, so please feel free to use your imagination when assembling your personal collection.

HAND SPANKING

Forgive me if I start with the absolute basics, but the male hand should never be overlooked in any discussion of the art of female bottom smacking. Besides the wonderful intimacy she experiences of being touched on the naked derriere by her revered teacher, there is also the convenience and almost spiritual simplicity of palm to buttock punishment. I like to believe that Adam did this to Eve. The naughty little bitch was naked, after all, and she certainly asked for it.

Personally, I regard a long, hot, over the knee session as

essential to warm up a girl's rear before proper exercise can begin, but I tailor the intensity of the smacks to the bottom being presented. My hands are so sharp that I can easily make most girls beg for mercy after only a dozen fierce and accurate handslaps, and we are only just getting started with whacking her hindquarters. Anyway, she has much worse to endure later on, so I generally begin with a large quantity of moderate, stinging tail smacks, just hard enough to wake up her bottom, and clear the wax out of her ears.

And of course, with empty hands, good hard bottom and anal pinches or painful tugs and stretches of the labia and clitoris (if they are dry enough) can be swiftly effected without interrupting the punishment rhythm. Keep a fresh jay cloth on hand so that if her genitalia do become too slippery to torment successfully, you can always give her a humiliating wipe down during the procedure.

Cunny honey is always rewarding to see and it adds a stimulating fragrance to any gymnasium, but it should not be allowed to interfere with proper persecution of her private places. Girls with copiously greasy snatches should be scolded for their disgracefully obvious state of arousal until they hang their heads in red-faced shame. I find making her bite down on an unacceptably soggy twat rag while I spank her to be a salutary lesson in self-control.

Whether or not you decide to administer formal otk handspankings during training, don't neglect to use your hands to slap her thighs, buttocks and pussy firmly, to punctuate your instructions as you guide her around the gym and position her on the apparatus. Remember that good slaps with the hand to intimate places are just as useful to reassure and steady her, or indicate that you approve of her performance, as they are to demonstrate your anger and point out failure.

Safety note: before you do smack her on the fanny, please read the guidelines on sensible practice with regard to genital slapping in Part 2 of this manual.

THE PLIMSOLL

As an enthusiast for all things educational, I like the school plimsoll to be an object of worship for my girl, and it really comes into its own during gym lessons. My punishment plimsolls are reinforced with a homemade heavy wooden insole so that they whack hard, making a lovely sound and vibrating her tush deeply right from anus to quim. The strokes can also be dragged so that the tread burns the cheeks like fire, generating a superb glow very quickly.

Obviously, it is an object that naturally belongs in the gymnasium, and has a fabulous and unique aroma fondly reminiscent of fit-bottomed females playing netball in their knickers. Great for six of the best, but for regular use, choose a black one that won't show up dusty fingerprints.

THE RULER

Another college favourite, this simple spanking utensil becomes more effective the more often you practice wielding it. The relatively small whacking surface means that you can punish small areas with fiendish accuracy to create localised hotspots, or beat her cheeks hard right down between the buttocks to redden even this normally inaccessible area. Masters who pride themselves on achieving that all over glow will need to use this precise instrument to tan those hard to reach places.

Handy hint: Explain all this to her while you're delivering the beating. Oh yes, and keep a spare on hand if you're using a wooden one, since they can snap with regular, intensive use.

THE TABLE TENNIS BAT

These sporty implements are cheap and easy to obtain and make nice circular scorches on her naked bottomflesh with flat, clean strokes. Some wrist strength is required to hit hard, but this means that with lesser force, longer, more leisurely whackings can be applied. It just looks so professional as well when delivered otk, so I recommend you use a gym mirror, so that both of you can admire your spanking form, and you can perfect your delivery as you administer the swipes. Keep your back straight, and start each stroke up high, well above the shoulder.

It also makes an excellent sound upon impact, and this combined with its gentler action makes it ideal for drawn out spankings when she needs recovery time across your lap between particularly strenuous exercises. Make her part her thighs so that you can pat her vulva with the bat edge-on whenever it tickles your fancy – not too hard, because if you line it up just right between the lips it's easy to make her inhale sharply and yelp with even minimal force. Great fun to use, and comes in a choice of attractive colours.

THE WOODEN SPOON

In a sporting context, anyone who finishes in last place is said to "get the wooden spoon" and so it seems wholly appropriate that your girl should be the recipient of this proverbial humiliation at least once when she fails to attain the impossible goals that you set for her during her exercise session. It's something a bit different and shows that you are proficient with a wide range of spanking instruments. Large, varnished salad spoons are the best for spanking because they are relatively heavy, tough, easy to clean and wow, do they pack a wallop!

Smaller, round handled spoons are ideal for unhurried and excruciating punishment insertions either up her bottom or vagina, but you will need to use lubricant unless you intend to inch it nice and slowly up a very moist quim. Vaseline is both convenient and relatively odourless, but the mildly antiseptic Savlon is also fairly inoffensive, and is quite soothing on sore orifices that have been recently violated.

Masters who like their female to feel the heat, can smooth their spoon's upward passage with tiger balm or Vic's vapour rub, or put a drop or two of Olbas Oil into the Vaseline. Be aware though that all of these can smell rather strong, and also hurt like the merry devil on her pinkskin, so don't go overboard unless you both know what you're getting into.

For such invasive procedures, you will need to buy a properly varnished spoon that can be thoroughly washed and disinfected after use.

Safety note: never use the same spoon for both holes, and never use the same spoon for two different girls. This is just basic hygiene. Also, take great care and proceed very gently when anally humiliating any girl who is not well used to this kind of debasing invasion. Never use force, since it can take time and practise for many women to learn to accommodate more than an inch or so of rectal penetration.

Handy hint: if you train more than one female, write her name and then either "anus" or "pussy" on the bowl of the spoon with indelible marker. Telling her which one to fetch from the drawer does something to a girl's tummy that is very difficult for them to put into words.

"Not enough effort girl! Bring me the pussy spoon. Oh, and the tiger balm, please!"

ANUS
PUSSY

THE PADDLE

This is a very severe one, but very cute and appropriate because the paddle I have for use on my female's behind is a delightful miniature wooden cricket bat about a foot and a half long including the handle. The bare wood is best applied to naked buttocks lightly, because it will harshly bruise and eventually break the skin if overused.

Girls do tend to love the look and feel of it though, because I have a second one with the flat blade coated with a layer of sticky felt so that I can safely beat them long and hard with it (at a pinch, a thin sock will serve as temporary insulation if you can't get hold of the felt or don't want to permanently soften your only paddle). The padded strokes are very deep and penetrating, like being kicked in the bottom with a soft, firm shoe, I'm told, and too much of that can make a squirty girl spray like a pony in heat. I kid you not, so be careful!

THE CANE

The proud prince of the pantheon of punishment props, the cane is the ultimate symbol of the gym master's authority and should always be visible to your girl during exercise, so lean it up against the door when you're not using it to orchestrate or punish. If it blocks the main exit from the gym it will strongly indicate your all-important "no escape" approach to the lesson.

In my home, my girl is forbidden to touch the cane unless I order her to fetch it, or use it upon her naked bum, the penalty being the severest whipping she can possibly conceive, and so hanging it from a door handle is as effective a deterrent as any lock.

Brandish it frequently, especially when she is bending over for you, and by all means apply the odd stroke during the session to keep her on her toes. (See the discussion of "striping" in Part 2 of this manual) Principally however, the proper moment for a full caning is at the end of the session, when she is exhausted and ready to be broken at your leisure.

If you like to perform this ritualised corporal crescendo in situ then, after exercise, bend her over a suitably large piece of furniture, like a vaulting horse (for apparatus junkies) or the back of a large chair (for make and menders). Alternatively, she can present on all fours for you, making her bottom a much more provocative target. This may require that she climb onto a low surface (coffee table height) so that her hindquarters are high enough for deep, level strokes to be applied.

To get this right, a good rule of thumb for achieving full and proper contact is that if you take a short step away from your caning stance in the opposite direction from her head, her anus and pussy should both be clearly visible when her knees are apart. This rule holds good even when she is on the floor: take the step back and then make her lower her head and shoulders to the floor (as though worshipping you). With her back sufficiently arched that you can see both rose and bud, return to your caning position. You can now deliver downward strokes to her upturned rear without losing penetration.

Of course, canings can always be administered to a standing girl, bent double, feet apart, holding her ankles if she's flexible enough, knees if she is not, but masters may find her leg trembling exhaustion to be a cause of frustration rather than delight if they expect her to be able to hold that position under a whipping after a very thorough training session. For very weary little pussycats, a whipping stool is favoured.

Personally I always prefer that we repair to my study so

that I can cane her in a formal and unhurried fashion after training her. Interestingly, by the time we get to this wonderful point in the proceedings, it almost never occurs to her to wonder why she is being subjected to this harsh additional punishment as a climax to my afternoon's recreation.

I think it just seems inevitable to her after such a protracted episode of scolding and spanking, that I should be driven by anger and disappointment to work off my frustration by throwing her over the whipping stool and beating the living daylights out of her with my bamboo bosom buddy.

At any rate, it is traditional for a girl to be caned after exercise. I tend to think of it as the most ruthless part of a well-earned detention after failing class. Besides, if I have not already spurted while putting her through her paces in the gym, it gives me a perfect opportunity to correct that omission with a badly needed emission, leisurely choosing either her vulva, rectum, bottom cheeks, face or mouth as depository for my royal mess.

CLOTHING

Let's turn now to the important matter of exercise attire. After the discussion above, it seems abundantly clear that a girl's backside needs to be bare during PT exercise. Some men prefer to make their girls strip completely before working them hard, enjoying the sound of bare feet on wood and the sight of liberated jumper bunnies bouncing in time to their commands. Others warm to the "gym kit with no shorts and knickers" look. Another favourite is the "buck naked with only gym shoes and white socks" uniform.

I enjoy all of these, and each is shamefully debasing in its own way. I do recommend though, that whatever style of undress you prefer, you always insist that your girl attends gym class fully dressed in proper kit. This means a spotless set of sports bra, t-shirt, tight shorts or lycra leggings, socks and trainers or pumps. Then you can enjoy instructing her just what to remove and in what order, and it allows you to change your mind at the last minute without appearing indecisive in front of your trembling wench:

"Shorts off, girl. I want to see your bare arse while I'm making you sweat."

"I think you'll be doing PT in the nude today, wench. Get your kit off."

"No knickers for you, lazy bitch. We're going to work that kitty bare this afternoon."

"You'll do as I say, and you'll do it all naked. Now strip!"

Now that you've got her undressed to your satisfaction, it's the perfect time to consider your own private parts.

Compelling a girl with smacks to perform rigorous exertions for my pleasure with her secret places shamefully exposed inevitably leads to a supercharged erection, and so what better way to enhance her degradation than to allow her to witness the provocative effect of her naked ordeal upon your sacred pole.

She will feel her shame more keenly as you become progressively stiffer, meaning that your proud rod will provide her with extra embarrassment directly proportional to your level of genital excitement.

Although I have heard tell of males who will conduct proceedings with no trousers on, or even in a total state of undress, my feeling is that this lessens the sense of inequality engendered by the nudity of her own delightful lower half. With this in mind, I simply neglect to don underwear when I change into my gym clothes.

The advantage of going commando like this is that if you

wear shorts or trousers with a fly, simply lowering the zip will liberate your aroused manhood swiftly and most visibly. This allows it to bob and twitch freely in front of her eyes, or be pressed threateningly against her bottom, pussy or thigh whenever she is ordered to assume a suitably vulnerable position.

When her tail is somewhat chilled by its exposure, and not yet fully warmed by repeated spanks, just the heat of your love club as it prods her soft places can be enough to provoke a quiet and anxious gasp.

In fact, should you require impromptu sexual relief at any stage, or merely want to keep her back straight, you can just step forward and plunge it right into her without any fumbling or delay. The startled scream that such unexpected penetration can elicit is a deeply exciting sound, sure to bring a smile to the face of even the sternest taskmaster.

Finally, men who consider themselves to be sufficiently buff to get away with it, can remove their shirts, but I prefer to reserve this for the hottest weather. There's just something about rolling up the sleeve of one's spanking arm that sets the tension appropriately high as you approach her bottom.

So, let's assume that you have your girl just as you want her: totally or partially naked with your throbbing maleness suitably rampant before her frightened eyes, and your treasury of spanking implements arranged within easy reach.

LET THE EXERCISE BEGIN!

Part 2 of this handy guide will contain detailed instructions for applying these instruments of correction to her bare bottom to maximise her efforts and simultaneously enhance your enjoyment of her physical education.

Also, thanks to the many requests I have received for guidance on the increasingly popular and delightfully knee-weakening art of female genital persecution, it will also include a brief, but thoroughly stimulating discussion of the finer points of safe and simple gymnasium techniques. I will explain how to patiently apply these excruciating torments to a girl's anus and pussy while seamlessly integrating them into her punishment training routine.

WHIPPING HER ARSE INTO SHAPE: PART 2

In Part 1 of this practical guide to the punishment training of lazy lasses, I restricted myself to outlining just the preparations required for a fully satisfying session of erotic exercise at the expense of your subordinate wench.

I am assuming that you have read this treatise in full, and having applied the instructions therein, are now in the proud and pleasing possession of the following:

1) A disciplinary arena, suitably large enough for not only her naked leaps and suggestive postures, but also with sufficient elbow clearance to allow unfettered swipes with the longest whipping stick you intend to use. As we say in my house, "Enough room to stretch a pussy and swing a cat."
2) One girl, totally or partially stripped to your customary tastes, taut and trembling as she tries to prepare herself to satisfy your sadistic appetite for her soft female body.
3) A selection of your favourite beating instruments for use on said girl's bottom thighs and quim, chosen for their aesthetic qualities (colours, shapes, impact sounds et cetera) catering to an appropriately wide range of whacking intensities.
4) A very large and almost painfully stiff erection, preferably clearly visible to your already humiliated and captive female audience of one.

LET THE SESSION COMMENCE!

Safety

A brief word on safety before starting Punishment Training: as with any form of exercise, start gently, especially if your winsome wench is no spring chicken, or is not yet in great shape. When thrashing a less experienced filly to fitness, for the first dozen workouts, you might want to try just putting her bare arse through the thoroughly degrading warm ups only, which are great fun in themselves. The even more demeaning and painful exercises can be added in gradually as you see fit and as the squealing squaw becomes more resilient, and firm of naked bottom.

Build up slowly, and it is far more likely that you will both still be enjoying the rigorous benefits and pleasures of regular PT a year, or even ten years from now, and just think how pert her taut little arse will be by then!

THE WARM UP

Warming up is an essential part of any healthy exercise regime and Punishment Training is no different in this respect. There's no point in rushing in and causing injury, and besides, the warm up can be every bit as heated and delicious as the full workout. Think of it as being rather like torturous foreplay: a gentle, teasing build up, but an essential part of good sex.

Now I've already mentioned that it is my preference to warm up a wench quite literally, with a good hard spanking over my knee, and that is in fact as good a place to start as any for men who like to get right down to bottom slapping business. For her part, it is a salutary reminder of just who is in charge during the session, gets her firmly into the obedience mindset, plus, it stiffens up my bare cock until it is twitching.

The trauma and embarrassment of being spanked on the bum will naturally get her blood flowing, and together with her gentle and helpless kicking, the resistance tensions in the spankee's muscles will loosen up her back, bottom and legs nicely. Make her plant her hands firmly on the floor and press hard to extend the warm-up into her neck and arms, stressing the whole of her taut and struggling body beautifully while you go to town on her back end. Smack slowly, and enjoy noisily covering the whole of her bottom and the sensitive backs of her thighs as many times as you can in two full minutes, pausing periodically to stretch your stiff cock to left and right and sigh, loudly. "Aaah!" The big man is going to be working hard throughout the session, so you need to wake up his muscles too!

MOTIVATIONAL SPANKS

Even if you decide to skip the preliminary spanking, you must not neglect the practice of constantly smacking her bottom and legs to control her performance during exercise. A suitable tempo of slaps of sufficient harshness will see target areas redden up pleasingly and very quickly once you get into the swing of non-stop chastisement, and should stay that way as long as you are working hard enough at the punishment.

Remember to smack her smartly before and after each instruction. Slap her bum, and say "No!" if she makes a mistake, smack her and say "Good!" if she gets it right. If she hesitates, whack twice and say "Quick quick!!" These wallops should produce a sharp sound, and aim to raise the prickly hairs on the back of her neck each time your palm finds its mark.

If that sounds like a lot of smacking, don't worry, it's meant to be! You'll soon fall into the rhythm, and if your fingers and hands start to sting then switch to the ruler. While slapping, aim for her bottom and thighs, the backs of her legs and if you can reach it easily and it's not too moist, the curve of her pussy.

Safety note: slapping her genitals should always be done more gently and very sparingly, usually with just the fingers rather than the palm. Firstly, it isn't easy to make a solid palm contact with the pussy except during stretches where you hold her on her back with her thighs splayed wide. Secondly, smacking the clitoris hard is ill-advised, because a bad bruise there is not going to be funny for either of your love lives. Committed tuppence tuggers will find it safer and more fun to squeeze, twist, pinch or stretch her love bud with just two fingers when it is being presented in an accessible position.

STRESS POSITIONS

When she stands up to rub her flaming cheeks after her initial spanking, it may be tempting to get her straight into star jumps or jogging on the spot, so that you can see her tits and freshly reddened ass bouncing like volleyballs at a beach party. Resist that urge, because you need to complete her warm up properly, and there are humiliating ways to do that that are gentler, but equally rewarding, perhaps more so.

I am referring here to the dreaded stress positions, which can not only be used to very effectively wake up her bare body to the prospect of vigorous exercise, but can also be utilised more sternly later on in the program, to reduce her quivering muscles to helpless jelly as the exercise session progresses. Take time to master these devilish ordeals, and you will come to delight in watching your naked girl endure them almost as much as she will come to fear them.

Tell her to fetch you the ruler and put her on her hands and knees on the floor in front of you. Now that you've got her nicely displayed on all fours at your feet with a whacking tool in your hands, you can explain the next stage of the warm up to her and be sure of her rapt and quivering attention.

"Right, my little bare-bottomed friend, we're going to do some stress positions. Keep your hands and feet on the floor and lift your naked rear end into the air. Quick, quick!" WHACK! WHACK!

By the way, it's better to use the ruler to administer instruction whacks during the stress positions. It's a good habit to get into because you'll need to sting her hard to make her obey later on, when she's tired. If you're really hooked on handslapping don't worry, you can go back to that for the full exercises later on in the programme.

"Keep pushing your bottom up. I want those legs straight. Good!" WHACK!

Handy hint: try this if your girl is inflexible in the hips or has tight hamstrings: After the motivational stroke, place your palm on her backside and press the heel of your hand firmly between her cheeks, below her straining anus, just at the point where you can see the pussy lips beginning to divide.

I learned this trick from a superb young filly who practised yoga. Your knowledge of her anatomical secrets will amaze her, since this pressure will help her to release the tension in her pelvic floor and allow her to keep her legs straight while she follows your next command:

"Now lift up onto your toes. Good!" WHACK!

You will have to remove your hand to slap her unless you are lucky enough to be an ambidextrous spanker, so after the encouragement stroke, replace it on her secret pressure point and push a little harder if necessary to help her right up onto her toes as you have ordered. You should be able to hear little noises of exertion coming from her, and her bare legs and bottom may tremble. This is the result you want.

This is a good place to leave your hand for a while, since if your girl has a very sensitive anus, you can amuse yourself by tapping it hard to make her gasp in time to your touch. This is a fascinating reflex to observe and besides, tickling her bum and privates while she is posing for you like this, forcing her hindquarters up into the air in front of you, will make her burn up with humiliation.

"Now hold that position, girl. Move an inch and it's six of the best!" WHACK!

Bear in mind that this position is costing her dearly. Therefore, when you are starting the warm up, let her down early, but after a half dozen or so repetitions, keep her up at full tension until her strength begins to fail and one of her legs bends slightly. Without hesitation scold her and give her a good, sharp six of the best with the ruler.

"I said don't move an inch, and I meant it! I'll skin your little arse if you so much as twitch it again!"

Keep a close eye on her feet because she should stay up on those toes the whole time. One or both heels will probably drop while she fights to keep her naked legs straight for you. Be ruthless and punish the slightest waver with another hackle-raising six. If it looks too easy for her, or you get bored, make her part her feet wider to make her wobble as she opens her pussy for you, and if you feel like a bit of extra fun, pinch or gently kick her bottom, or tweak her vulva to make her fail and collapse to her knees.

You can also try tickling her bottom and flanks to weaken her. I used to train a wench who would actually scream blue murder as she tried to keep her position while I ran my fingers quickly over her bare back and thighs. That was a most gratifying response.

If you are lucky enough to own a very ticklish bitch like this, you can stand behind her while she holds her quivering ass high, and place your erection lengthways between her buttocks. When you tease her bottom and flanks with your fingers, her desperate, but restricted bucking action will quickly and erratically bounce her hips up and down, masturbating you most effectively with her bottom crack.

Positioning yourself just right for this can take a bit of practise and she will need to be taught to cooperate somewhat. Skinny wenches may need to squeeze their cheeks together to some extent, but squaws with deeper cleavages can just focus the tension in their lower thighs to generate short, sharp burst of power, and guarantee you a very satisfying wank.

As I have pointed out, you may want to come back to stress positions later between the exercises, and there are various ways to augment this already very degrading process. Try the following:

TIP 1: THE FANNY CRANE

Get her ass in the air and tie a small rope – about a quarter inch diameter or less – around her waist, take the free end and bring it up between her buttocks so that it uncomfortably bisects her pussy lips. This is called a "fanny-crane". Make her lift onto her toes when her feet are tired, by pulling the rope, upwards and slightly towards her head.

Only gentle tugging is needed to add an extra ear-popping dimension of bottom-twitching, clit-squeezing, pussy-biting wedgie pain to the exercise, and it makes dropping her feet utterly impossible. She'll beg for a whacking sooner rather than later, just to ease the pressure on her straining twat. This can be excruciating teasing for her, so consider giving her something to bite on for protracted lifts and always let her down as soon as she submits.

TIP 2: TWAT ZAPPING

Alternatively, if you have a TENS unit, you might want to insert an electric probe into her anus (make sure it's a shaped one that will not be involuntarily expelled by the stress of her posture) and a larger one into her vagina, or else attach electro clips to her labia. These items are quite pricey but a worthwhile investment if recreation requires you to regularly torment your lass anyway.

In stress positions, bottom or leg twitches and loss of tension in her aching muscles can be rewarded with a bolt of lightning to the private place of your choice. Just a few volts will feel like she's having red-hot pokers pushed up her bum and fanny, but despite the intense pain, it's completely safe and leaves no mark whatsoever. It's genius really, and you'll be amazed at the reserves of stamina you will help her to discover in this way.

Handy hint: Always keep the probes on a low voltage between the big zaps, and the involuntary muscular contractions that result will keep her sphincters nice and tight, holding the lightning rods firmly in their little pink holes, until you decide to turn up the heat.

As a variation, you can just keep her with her bare bum skyward, attach a full complement of electrodes, and play "eeny-meeny-miney" with the shock treatment. You may find this quite an addictive game in itself, and as a man who like to pass the time by tormenting his girl, I've made my wench endure this in the bedroom more often than the gym.

Getting back to exercise though, my suggestion is that you return to stress positions throughout the workout, progressing through the augmentations as you get more excited by her distress. For example, warm her up with a few gentle reps of the basic stress position, then later in the workout, get her back into this position, and torment her harder and longer by spanking her raised arse while spicing things up with a little twat tweaking. Her third set can involve some eye-watering fanny-crane elevations, and then you can finish the workout with a draining ordeal of electrically enhanced motivation before she abjectly whimpers for mercy, collapses completely, and you drag her off by the scruff of her neck for a well-earned caning.

But for now, let's get back to describing the end of the warm up stress positions. Her strength has just failed for the first occasion, so it's time to absolve her of her naked shame, and make her run and fetch you the plimsoll.

You need a reasonably sturdy, hard backed chair to sit on while you're formally spanking her, and a light one that can easily be moved around is a great advantage since she's going to be taking it on the ass here, there and everywhere around the gym. At this early stage, she just needs a short, sharp walloping – six of the best is usual with the plimsoll in our house - and a good telling off for being such a pathetic weakling.

"That was rubbish!" WHACK! "You're a lazy little cow!" WHACK! "And lazy little cows get their arses beaten!" WHACK! "What are you?" WHACK! "Say it!" WHACK! "That's right! Pathetic!" WHACK!

And so on.

Do make sure that she knows she's being thrashed for disappointing you, and that she'll be beaten again after each exercise, with a venom and duration that depends solely upon how satisfied you are with her achievements. Let her also know that you expect her to howl, beg and vow to do better next time while she's receiving these motivational whackings.

THE MAIN WORKOUT
JOGGING AND JIGGLING

She's now ready for the eagerly anticipated star-jumps or running on the spot, and though you may enjoy watching, and adopting a casual demeanour while she bounces and jiggles her unclothed assets for your amusement and pleasure, don't appear too idle or she may start to relax. You want to keep your pony leaping high over the hedges, and it's vital to keep her bare body sweating!

Occasional hard smacks to the bottom with hand or ruler will let her know the score, and bark short, sharp commands "Higher, wench!" (for star jumps) or "Keep those knees up, bitch!" (for running on the spot) as you whack. "I want to see those jugs bouncing, girl!" You will be enjoying this, but she mustn't.

As she gives up in mewling despair, or you merely become dissatisfied with her erotic performance, it's back to the chair for another lovely formal punishment. She'll be panting hard, and hopefully perspiring sweetly, so I'd recommend giving her a breather by means of a longer, exciting beating with a lighter implement – say thirty strokes of the table tennis bat.

Spanking a girl when she's already out of breath makes the whole thing sound much more stirring, and that, together with the added tang of pussysweat in the air will make you want to whack her forever. Therefore, I suggest you make her count the blows so that you don't get lost, and so that you can lecture her, scold her, and nurse your raging hard-on without losing track of the bigger numbers. This is deeply humiliating for any girl, and if she makes a numerical mistake, then start the whole punishment again. She won't repeat the error.

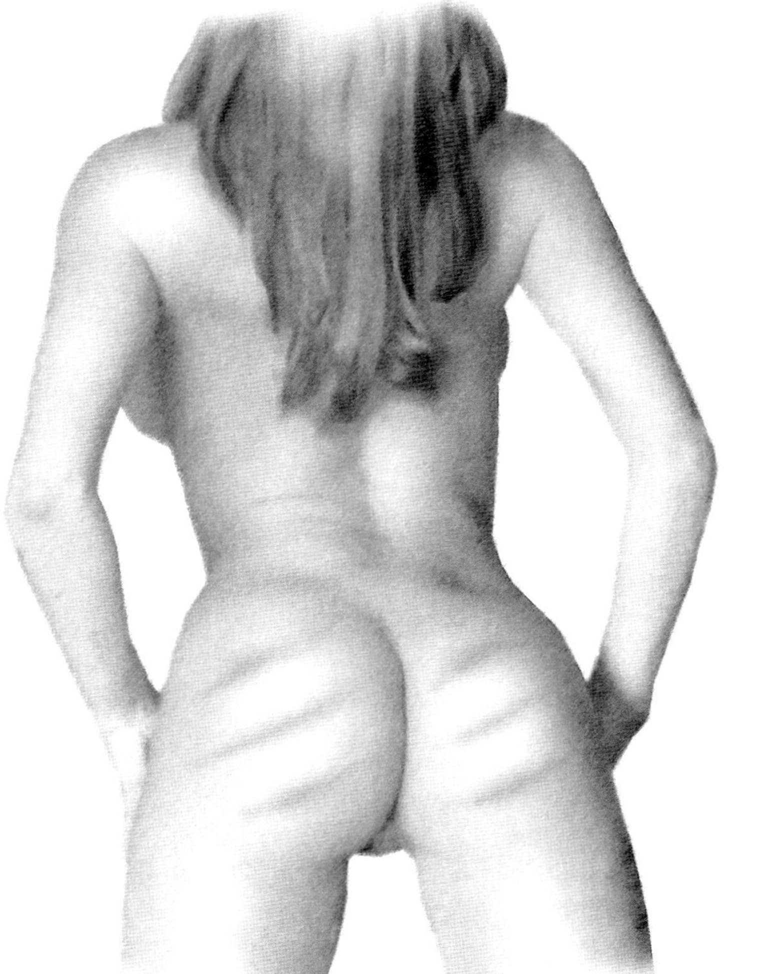

LET'S MOVE ON TO SOME MORE ADVANCED EXERCISES.

I'm going to assume that if you have specialised exercise equipment, then you know how to use it, and I don't intend to put off first time gym masters by harping on about expensive workout props that are of no interest to the beginner. Instead I'll outline some exercises that are easy to do either with improvised apparatus or free standing, and that should give the gizmo junkies among you all the hints they need to adapt the punishment motivation techniques to their own more sophisticated tastes.

STEPS

Any low bench or step will do, but don't use books or a washing up bowl because they will slip dangerously. Avoid surfaces that are too high, like a chair, because she may well trip, fall and hurt herself. Anything that results in an injury more serious than a sore bottom, an aching pussy or deeply bruised self-esteem should be very carefully avoided.

She must step up onto the bench with her left foot, then quickly follow it with the right. The left foot then steps back down, followed by the right again. Start her slow and then quickly build up to a fast rhythm.

Two approaches to delivering excellent motivational punishments while she puffs and pants are applicable to many of these exercises and I will mention them both here.

QUICKSLAPPING

Firstly you can select a light implement, such as the ruler, take up a stance behind her and whack her smartly on the bottom each time both of her feet are on the floor. This recurring and regular application of bare arse smacks, harmonised with her exertions is called "Quickslapping".

Obviously, this is very stimulating, but also quite tiring for you and requires some concentration if she is exercising at speed, but you can with a little practise build up a lovely synchronistic rhythm that becomes almost meditative over a period of minutes, as her arse begins to redden and burn like fire, and she howls in time to the echoing sound of the spanks. Furious and excited whacking like this will work wonders for your own conditioning, so you should at least give it a try.

STRIPING

Alternatively, more sedate males may select a more severe instrument, say the cane or paddle, and deliver an occasional, piping hot stroke to her straining cheeks: "Faster, wench!" to boost her flagging energy levels. This is known as "striping".

Again, healthier bitches can be led from one whacking tempo to the other during the same session. Start with a casual striping rhythm, and then as she starts to seriously tire, angrily declare that you're going to have to take proper charge of the situation, fetch the ruler and turn up the pressure with an exciting minute or two of Quickslapping to squeeze some extra ounces of effort out of her perspiring naked body.

When she fails or surrenders, play the punishment spanking by ear, and vary the length and intensity of these beatings as much as you feel is appropriate. If she's very tired, you might take her otk for a leisurely hand or batspanking, but if she's just goofing off and still seems to have plenty of energy, then roasting her buttocks soundly with ten bites of the paddle is a more fitting reward.

Spooning is always a good option for accurate, scorching castigation, and will make you feel like a true professional, so don't forget that you have that weapon in your arsenal if you decide to give her a shorter, fiercer beating, or just want to shove something besides your erection up her fanny or bottom.

PRESS-UPS AND SQUATS

These are the traditional "superstars" exercises, and are really only for strong girls. I recommend that even with Amazonian females, you use "cheating" press-ups, which are done on the hands and knees. These are far less demanding and make her raised tail easier to beat. Both press-ups and squats present her soft bottom quite low, so you will probably need to kneel or sit next to her while she performs for you. This makes caning her bare tail more cumbersome, so use a paddle if you're laying on the harsher, striping strokes.

For those of you who don't know what a "squat" is, the girl gets down into the lovely all fours position, but unusually she is made to balance on her hands and feet, with knees bent, rather than going right down onto her hands and knees. This is such a great, pussy-pouting posture, that I make my girl adopt it just for punishment around the home. Making her hold this difficult pose while I ride her long and hard makes her wail wonderfully with distress. But I digress.

Next, order her to bring her knees right up against her elbows (or as near as she can get them). She must then, keeping her palms on the ground, push or jump her feet back in one movement until her legs are almost straight out behind her. Bringing the knees back again, in a single jump or slide, to the squatting position, completes the movement. No girl can effect this taxing exertion without grunting in a most pleasing fashion. It's a hard cock noise that always makes me smack her bottom and laugh.

Most girls can push out a lot more squats (or squat thrusts) than they can press-ups, and they present her rear end in a more convenient fashion for spanking. The optimum point to deliver the stroke is in the start-finish position, when the squaw's bare bot will be stationary, slightly raised upward, rounded and full.

If you're a committed Quickslapper, permit her to push out another squat, only after you have whacked her hard on the ass. This is the signal for her to go again and in this way you can control the speed of her routine, and when she is nearing exhaustion, give her another reason to dread your inevitable scorching swipe across her buttocks.

SQUAT JUMPS

A more advanced variation on the squat and this really is only for quite athletic young fillies. After completing the basic thrust on all fours, make the girl stand up and jump in one smooth movement, bringing her knees up high and touching her shins briefly with her fingertips. On landing, she must drop down into the squatting position to perform another thrust.

For maximum satisfaction, punish with a Quickslapping rhythm, but make her wait in the squat position for the whack on her rear just prior to her leap, and as you deliver the cut, shout: "Jump!"

This teaches her, quite literally, that when you say jump,

she jumps. A little obvious perhaps, but a bedrock principle of mastery that ought to be drilled into her until it becomes instinctive. Again, use the Quickslapping to regulate the speed of her performance. Since you will have to stand or sit slightly behind her to administer the whipping effectively, make sure that mirrors are appropriately positioned, so that you get a good view of her baps as they fly through the air with the greatest of unease.

If you ever want to hear your girl, quite literally cry out with exertion, then these squat jumps are something to work towards. It's a sound you will always recall with a stiff plonker.

SKIPPING

The swinging rope obviously makes concurrent punishment impossible, but the display of nude female assets bouncing at speed is incomparable. If she can't skip, laugh at her blushes out loud while she learns. Between sound failure beatings, sit back, reprimand and enjoy.

SIT-UPS

Every girl should be vigorously encouraged to develop a six-pack, and she can certainly flatten that stomach, provided she is compelled to perform her crunches regularly. Put her on her back on the floor or exercise mat, make her put her hands behind her head and draw her knees up towards her chest. Remember that even if she knows the ropes, it never goes amiss to guide her into position yourself, judiciously smacking sensitive places all the while.

Kneeling beside her hips, her pussy will be within easy

reach. Tap it or pinch – whichever you prefer, as you explain the requirements of the exercise. Adjust your technique to keep her focussed and alert, being aware that if she climaxes involuntarily, she may not be able to continue.

The basic crunch is performed by raising her head towards her knees. You are probably now addicted to Quickslapping, so you can either stimulate her to begin each rep with a whack across her nicely presented cheeks and thighs, or alternatively make her hold the crunch at full tension, bottom upturned, until you wallop her. This latter variation has the interesting effect of making her long for the release stroke once her tummy muscles start to burn.

You can of course do both: "Up!" WHACK! "Hold…! And down!" WHACK! This is called "Double Quickslapping" or more usually "Doubleslapping" and very controlling males will just love getting to grips with this sophisticated whackery.

Just be careful not to inadvertently whack the pussy while you're experimenting. The sight and scent of the bare and straining female crotch are pretty mesmerising in this position, and a wallop intended for the bottom should not be dragged off course by your eyes or nose into this softer and more tender, fragrant target, particularly if you are applying a harsh implement across her naked skin.

There is an easy way to avoid such a mishap, and masters addicted to such pervery will greatly enjoy seeing how many reps she can complete with a wooden spoon in each of her private holes. Gripping desperately onto those little poles to prevent their involuntary expulsion and hence a spanking will work wonders for her internal muscles, whilst protecting her vulnerable areas from oblique strikes intended for her bottom cheeks or thighs.

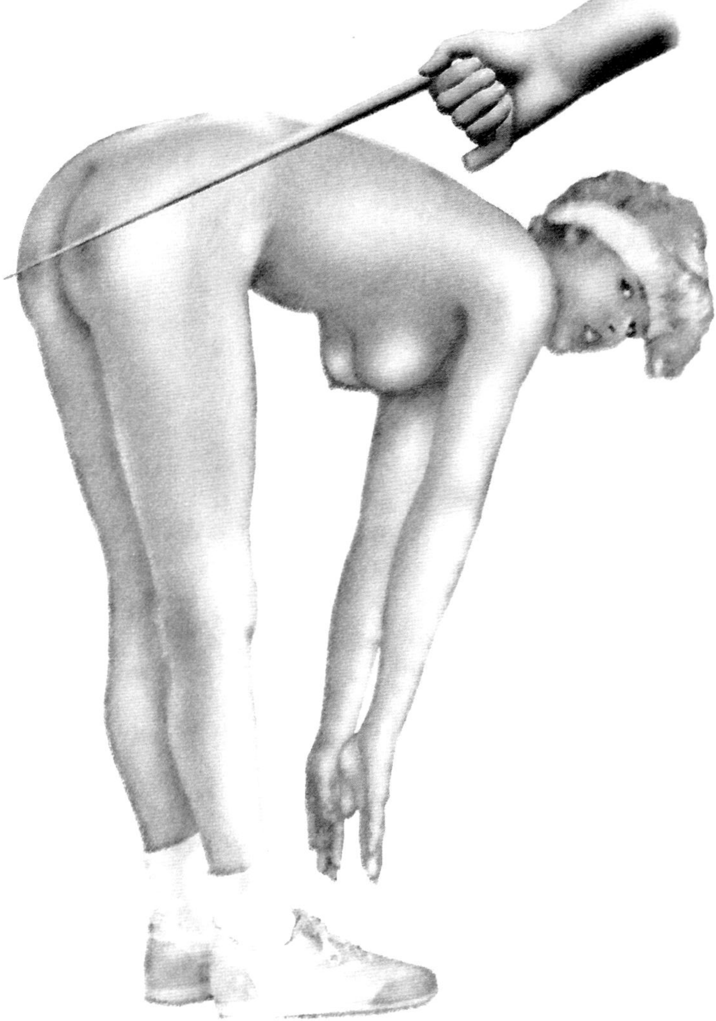

CIRCUIT TRAINING

A real favourite with all older men, since you get to sit and do nothing but whip bare ass. Fitter males will also see it as a great way to get their own breath back while they grind her down some more. Set up a small training course so that it includes several exercises and sit in your spanking chair. Let's say that exercise one is ten bottom raises into the basic stress position. Order her to begin and then verbally control her desperate exertions with slow and whimsical precision. When she has completed the set to your deep satisfaction, demand that she must sprint to the next exercise.

In restricted indoor space this running can be done on the spot right in front of you. In fact, I find this so appealing that even when running a girl outdoors, I make her jiggle in place before me for a portion of each sprint. I like to sit forward and apply motivational whacks while she gives me a slow, pneumatic twirl. As she jogs for me, I count to ten, marking time by smacking her thighs and bottom from different angles with both hands.

After jogging, exercise two might be twenty hops onto the stepping bench. Unable to exercise close control from your comfy chair, you must again motivate her with voice commands:

"Move those buns, you bare arsed little witch!"

"I want to see those jubblies jumping like salmon!"

"Put your bottom into it, or I'll beat you for an hour!"

Then send her on another hip-slapping cross-country-on-the-spot, before dropping her into the squat position. Your girl must execute ten squats flawlessly while you enjoy her involuntary genital display, and scold and ridicule her ruthlessly.

"Push those hips out, girl! I want to see you piss!"

"Precision, wench, precision! You'll keep those damn feet together when you've got my cock up your pink arse!"

Now there's just time for yet harder thigh whacking as she runs off some more calories in front of you before she has to race over to fetch the first piece of punishment equipment.

She must collect implement number one – usually the softest so let's go with the table tennis bat. Then it's straight over to your warm and waiting lap, whereupon she must present herself for the first spanking of say twenty strokes.

While she dutifully counts out loud in time to your disciplinary pleasure, this is your chance to press that hard-on against her pumping bottom, and explain in an angry voice that her efforts were less than the hundred and ten percent you had naturally expected:

WHACK! "You call that a circuit, you bare-bottomed wimp?" WHACK!

WHACK! "I want to smell some real painsweat on your pretty legs next time, girl!" WHACK!

WHACK! "Now shake your arse around that course again, and don't let me down again or else next time you're across my knee I'll spank your pussy!" WHACK!

Then she must start with exercise one – the stress positions – all over again. Everything is the same, the exercises, the jogging and the sound, barebottom spankings. The only differences is that she's getting more hopelessly fatigued, more wet, sexually excited and deeply embarrassed, and each time she completes a circuit, she must collect a progressively more severe whipping tool, before getting promptly over your knee to receive a darn good hiding, and a severe dressing down.

This is a very effective way to break a girl in to proper discipline, and it provides a natural way to escalate the punishment towards the climactic pinnacle of the traditional caning finale.

TIP 3: REALLY ADVANCED STUFF

Though I am not an expert wrestler, a few years ago, I picked up enough judo to enable me to enjoy working a girl on the mat, wringing every ounce of resistance out of her naked body until she is reduced to a trembling jelly of exhaustion, after which I can subject her to excruciating bouts of submission wrestling.

I will usually pin her down, put her in an arm or leg lock, or maybe a groin stretch if she is particularly weak in that area. I then apply unbearable pressure to an intimate nerve centre: the clitoris, g-spot or labia being obvious ones, but there are lesser known but equally valuable weaknesses just above and below the anal bud, and much of the soft skin that covers the buttocks is susceptible to carefully targeted and intense pinching.

I like to slowly increase the stress until, knees shaking for relief, she is forced to yield, while I tease her ruthlessly for her female weaknesses, and her embarrassingly moist cleft, which as before, I periodically dab with my pussywipe to enable better purchase for my tormenting fingers.

"Oh, look at this soggy mess, you filthy girl! Let's wipe this off, so that I can get another good firm pinch of that place again, because it did make you squirm, didn't it?"

"There now. Ooooooh,.... That's got to really hurt....And again, now: one, two three, wait for it... oooohhh... feel the burn, baby. Feel the burn!"

After each capitulation, she duly receives a beating in

direct proportion to her lack of fortitude, before being put into another agonizing and embarrassing position, to endure for as long as she possibly can.

Obviously, only skilled practitioners should attempt wrestling takedowns, and besides, strictly speaking, inflicting gratuitous pain in this way does not fall into the domain of everyday Punishment Training. It's more of a bedroom hobby. But once you've whipped your sub into really great shape, intimate physical domination of that kind is extremely good for both her mind and her soft little body.

Incorporating it into a weekly workout is something for ambitious men to aim for.

IN CONCLUSION

So whether you opt for a simple PT regime for your wench, or decide to subject her to a more elaborate programme of physical domination and humiliation, I would urge all masters to consider some form of degrading exercise for their females that goes beyond the everyday demands of housework, and domestic sexual servitude.

The benefits of vigorously working her under the whip, physically persecuting her into submission, and then ruthlessly and intimately tormenting her at close quarters should never be underestimated. It brings a girl into closer spiritual union with her superior male being, and keeps her young, strong, obedient and vital.

It's also great fun for you.

Now that you have put your shivering filly through her humiliating paces, don't forget to refer to the two chapters entitled "Cane your girl with confidence". There I describe how to administer that final beating after exercise, fully utilising the finer points of caning the female rear. There you will find many detailed pointers to help you to deliver accurate and bottom scorching strokes with this most traditional and venerated whipping accessory whilst using her extreme distress under punishment to maximise the intensity of your own sexual release.

Happy whacking.

THE SPANKING BUNNY HUNT

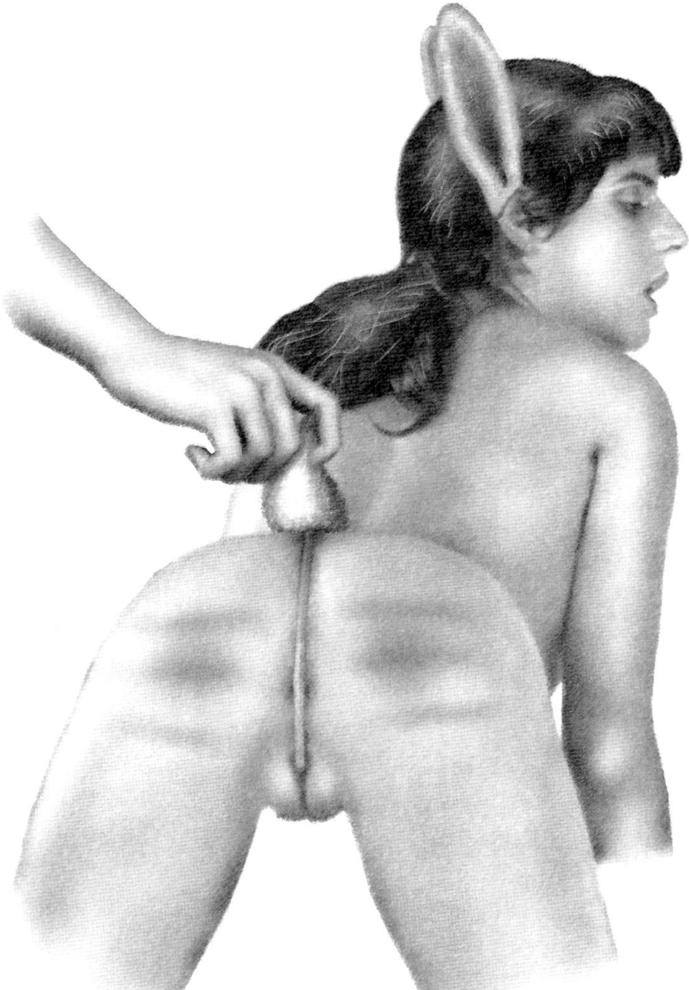

Note: despite the frequent references to skinning and eating of bunnies in this chapter, no rabbits were hurt during the researching of this material. As for the girls... well, their limits were fully explored.

As spanking royalty, I consider it to be an important duty of mine to educate others less fortunate than myself in the proper methods of female punishment. In this short missive, I intend to give a glimpse into how we, the corporal punishment aristocracy enjoy our rightful power over our women while relaxing and at play.

As you are aware, field sports form an indispensable part of the recreation of the higher classes, and as a member of the first family of punishment, and heir to the whipping throne of England, they are a regular duty of mine. Hence I consider that one of the finest ways to spend an afternoon in the company of one's subordinate girl is to organise a traditional bunny hunt.

For this you will need at least one submissive female, but there is actually no upper limit to the number of bare bottoms that can be tormented in this most agreeable game. Large hunting meets may regularly employ up to twenty bunny girls, but such sizeable flocks will require similarly large packs of men to chase them down, to ensure that each bunny is eventually caught. That said, this is also a delightful sport for a man to indulge in at home, should he desire a divertingly different way to privately tease his personal spanking wench.

Each female should be provided with a set of floppy bunny ears and a bunny tail. Opinions differ as to how much additional clothing should be worn, and many men understandably favour naked bunnies. I am a big fan of the tight t-shirt and also enjoy the sight of a lithe bunny girl ready to run in only a sports bra, stockings and suspenders, but whatever the dictates of fashion, hunting tradition demands that at the very least, proper bunnies should always be bare below the waist, with their private parts clearly visible and properly shaved to their masters' taste.

When running bunnies in a flock, socks are hygienically advised (and also cute!), and trainers are simply de rigueur if the bunnies are to be chased out of doors.

Bunny tails come in two different varieties. The first is simply an elasticated waist strap complete with fluffy attachment, the other, the so-called pullable tail, is an altogether more robust arrangement. It consists of a small leather belt, with a thong attached at the front. This is looped up between the legs, inserted between the lips of the pussy, and then brought up tight between the buttocks and tucked under the belt again at the back. The fluffy tail appendage is secured to this free end of the thong.

The thong should be thin enough to be prised between the girl's nether lips, but also thick enough to easily cover the sensitive clitoris as well as cause some uncomfortable separation of her labial folds. This ensures that that when her little tail is pulled, the resulting wedgie can be made as embarrassing and potentially painful as her tormentor desires.

Bunnies sporting pullable tails are naturally considered to be "asking for it" and large meets are often characterised by frequent squeaks and squeals of alarm as spectators and hunters alike, avail themselves of every opportunity to keep such bunnies literally "on their toes".

Pulling a bunny's tail can become rather an addictive habit, and it is well known that many a man who regularly hunts her, also secretly enjoys long evenings at home with his naked bunny over his knee, yanking that little tail until the poor little rabbit's hindquarters tremble like a shapely trifle. But I digress.

At the start of the hunt, the bunnies should line up side by side on all fours. This makes for a great deal of competitive bottom wiggling, and hence a very pretty spectacle indeed, with all those fluffy tails and pussies in the air. For this reason, the official photographer usually takes a souvenir snap at this point, and girls desiring anonymity can simply face front to protect their identities.

Feisty flocks should then be marshalled into order with judicious whacks from a cane or crop. They should be whipped hard enough to settle and quiet them, without making them jump up from the line. A dedicated steward may be required to keep control of the girls, since the male officiating as starter is himself required to hold the starting pistol in his whipping hand.

The so-called starting pistol is actually a hard slipper or plimsoll, used, because in the hands of a skilled operator, it can be brought swiftly across a girl's bare bottom to make a sound remarkably like a gunshot.

As each bunny's number is called, she must keep her hands and feet on the floor, but raise her hips as high as she can. After an appreciative pause, the starter will apply a stern whack to those temptingly raised hindquarters while he shouts out a series of commands:

"Bunny Number One, raise your tail!"

"Ready? Wait for it... wait for it..."

WHACK!

OWWW!

"Go, Bunny Number One!"

The first bunny should then sprint away clutching her bare bottom, and find a place to hide.

This delightful procedure is repeated to launch all of the

bunnies to flight, and should spectators be present, a round of applause should accompany each girl's humiliating send off.

When all the bunnies are away, then the hunters gather within earshot of their quarry and must threateningly intone the bunny hunter's refrain:

Fee, fie, foe, fum,
I smell the scent of a bunny girl's bum,
Just how squirmy will that bunny girl be,
While I skin her across my knee?

Squeamish vegetarians need not throw up their hands in horror. None of the bunnies are literally skinned. In the bunny hunt, "skinning the bunny" is a red-blooded euphemism for the sound spanking of a poor girl's bare behind. Also, don't worry if you feel a bit silly saying the rhyme. Everyone feels a little self-conscious at first. Just remember, this is a grand tradition, and once you get the hang of it, the silliness gets unbearably exciting.

You must split up to effectively hunt for the bunnies, and when you think one is nearby, you are advised to utter the bunny hunter's refrain again, this time whispered low and slow. You'd be surprised how often it makes them whimper, or break cover to give their hiding place away.

When you are certain you know where she is, you must shout, "Bunny on the run!" before you run her to ground. Even if you're not sure exactly where she is, you can sometimes flush her from cover just by shouting this.

Hunting methods vary between men, but most often, a bunny is caught by touching or smacking her bottom, or by grabbing her with both arms round the waist. Personally, I like to manhandle my captive, because I can go straight from there to hauling her over my knee into the “skinning position”. If you are lucky enough to scent a bunny with a pullable tail, grab hold of that and she will have no choice but to totter gingerly in whichever direction you steer her naked hips.

These are the instructions for holding your captured bunny down while you skin her. They assume that you are right handed. Lefties should simply reverse them. Make sure that the bunny is held down firmly on your lap by wrapping your left arm around her waist. Just like in the rhyme, I like my bunny to squirm while I’m skinning her, but at no point should she feel able to wriggle free from her ordeal.

Push your left knee between her thighs and use your left leg to pin her right one. Then bring your right calf over the back of her left leg and use it to pull her thighs apart. This separates the buttocks nicely for skinning. If you lean forward, you should be able to clearly see your bunny’s pussy. If not, she needs to arch her spine more. A compliant bunny will do this when instructed, but you may need to pinch the anus or clitoris of a more recalcitrant rabbit to make her obey.

Obedience aside, many hunters enjoy tormenting their prey in this intimate fashion for a while before skinning it anyway. Legend has it that such prolonged suffering makes the flesh taste sweeter, and anyway, it’s excellent fun.

Of course if your bunny has a pullable tail, it will need to be removed before you can turn your attention to the delicate pink secrets beneath. Dedicated tail tuggers will realise however that this is a golden opportunity to give her a very protracted lesson in their craft and if you believe the gourmet myth mentioned above then you will need to twist that tail like you mean it.

To skin your bunny, you will need a favourite skinning

implement. I use a twelve inch plastic ruler – cheap but effective. It's light and easy to carry during the chase, stings like a bitch across a girl's naked bottom cheeks, and makes a wonderful

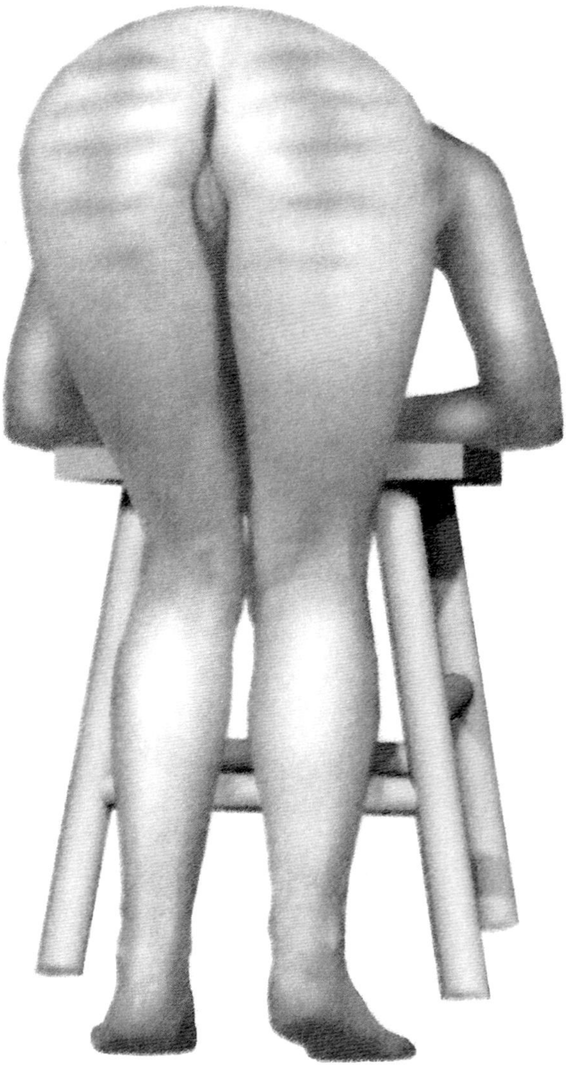

whacking noise that quickens even the hardest erection for the duration of a prolonged skinning. It also leaves a nice, rosy glow with no bruising so that the bunny knows she's been well and truly skinned, but she can also be sure that the nice red markings will fade long before her wonderful memories do.

Verbally tormenting your helpless bunny is an important part of the skinning ritual, and should be mastered in front of a mirror in private so that you can do it justice on the day without faltering. Styles vary, but I like to build up to the skinning with phrases like; "I'm going to skin you so, so slowly, little bunny", "I'm going to flay you inch by inch while you whimper and squeal", "Oh, this is going to hurt". You get the idea.

An experienced bunny skinner will want to carefully whack every inch of that lovely, vulnerable, quivering bunny's arse, and this is another advantage of my special ruler. With the end I can get right down between the cheeks, up under the undercurves, and even tan the small of her back. I also like to take time out to warm up her thighs individually and finish off by slowly whacking her pussy. I've had outdoor bunnies wet themselves on the grass while I tested their limits and scorched their secret places to boiling point. Oh what halcyon days!

Keep talking, that's my advice, particularly if you like your bunny to wriggle and squeak while she's being skinned. "Does that hurt, bunny girl?" "Don't you like being skinned, little bunny rabbit?" "Well I'm enjoying it!" "This is going to last a long, long time." "That's a sensitive bit, isn't it? We'll have to work on that bit for a while, won't we?" "Oooh, that's got to burn!"

When you feel that your poor little bunny has been well and truly stripped of her fur, then the final act of skinning is, if she still has one, to remove that little tail that's been bobbing up and down all the while she's been struggling. That's yours. A trophy to remind you of an excellent afternoon's hunting. If you live with your bunny, hang that little fluffy tail up somewhere around the house where she can see it, or once a week, make her wear just that and nothing else while she irons a pair of your socks for half an hour.

Now I know what some of you are going to say, hunting little bunny rabbits is cruel. And while I agree that it most certainly is extremely cruel and therefore highly enjoyable, I must also point out that we of the spanking upper crust are not mindless sadists – no! There are strict rules that govern any hunt, and the most important one is this: whatever you catch, you must eat.

Having skinned your bunny and removed its little tail, many of the more visceral members of the hunting fraternity are quite ready to lay that little bunny out on its back and eat it raw. I can see the appeal of such carnivorous lust, but I must say, I prefer my rabbit flesh well cooked before I tuck in.

And as far as I'm concerned, there's only one way to cook a freshly caught and skinned wild rabbit.

Spit roast.

AFTERWORD: BORN TO SPANK

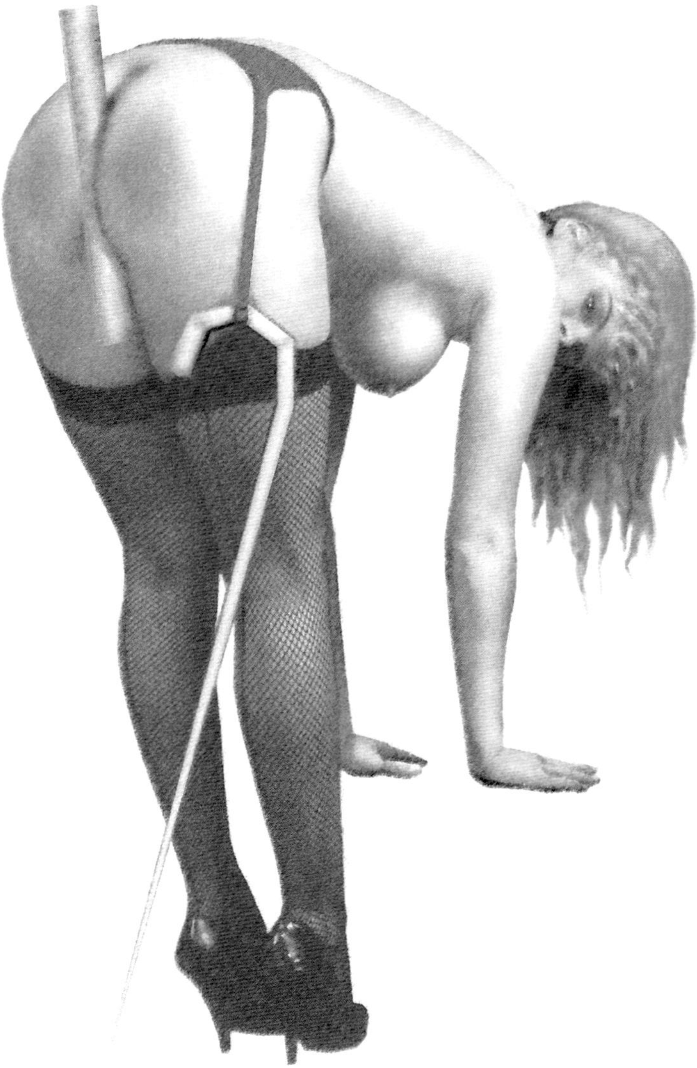

Being a man made famous by his predilection for the punishment of females for the purposes of both discipline and relaxation, people often ask me why it is that I so enjoy the spanking the fair sex.

No one puts this question to me more often and more mischievously than my subordinate female companion, knowing full well that my answer will begin with the words:

"Let me show you, dear"

I would then normally proceed to test the acoustics of the room with an ascending set of piercing feline squeals, released from her front end by an accurate series of increasingly hard whacks to her naked rear, and finish with the domineering flourish that we in the literary professions refer to rather loftily as "a bloody good shafting".

When I subsequently state, while zipping up my fly to restrain my fading erection: "I think I've made my point rather eloquently" I am yet to hear further dissent beyond a rather weary intonation to her utterance of the obligatory "Yes, Sir, thank you, Sir," that our post coital customs demand.

To the public at large, however, I feel that some lengthier explanation may be required, beyond the simple statement that sums up the whole subject for me in a mere five words:

I love beating girls' bottoms.

This is something that goes back a long way for me. When I was a wee lad at infant school I used to fantasise about watching my little friend Rosemary getting the slipper on her bare bum for being naughty, while I peeped round the door, breathing hard with a funny knot in my tummy.

Of course, I didn't really know what a girl's bottom looked like in those days and I had to use my naive and childish imagination to conjure it all, but now that I am a man, the naked tails of the fully grown and shapely women that I love to spank are far more exciting than anything than I could have dreamed of in my impish, innocent youth.

Evolution obviously fashioned the female hindquarters to attract the sexual attention of the male: those sweet, plump and rounded cheeks framing the sly and musky promise of her soft, beckoning pussy. Yet not content with this masterpiece of erotic design, nature and fate have somehow conspired to make punishment of her delectable rear the safest and most effective means to discipline a naughty girl.

No matter how soft and full the curve of her lovely hips may be, the foundations of every wench's derriere are firm and strong. The muscles of the buttocks are the largest and most powerful in the human body, making her presented arse the safest place to land corrective smacks with vigour and intent.

Yet despite the structural ease with which it can accommodate a good whacking, her bottom is more richly supplied with nerve endings than almost any other part of the surface of her skin, making lessons applied to it feel very sharp indeed. This ensures that whatever points you choose to emphasise by smacking her tender backside, will harshly stick in the notoriously selective female memory for the longest possible time.

Marry these happy accidents of natural selection with the equally delightful coincidence that the easiest way to restrain a woman completely with one hand is to hold her over your knee, and you make the wonderful discovery that while delivering a bare bottom spanking you have the perfect firm, helpless and sensitive target for punishment, as well as the most intoxicating sexual display.

The overwhelmingly private exhibition of prize pink, secret eye-candy and the hot and sensuous vapours of painsweat and scent leaking from her pouting split, merge with her giddying squeals of helpless despair and her exciting, pointless wriggles to launch an unbearably erotic assault on four of the senses of the fortunate man charged with the happy duty of punishing a pretty girl. And the fifth can be indulged at any point in the proceedings desired, simply by dipping a finger into that boiling, rich honey pot of female heat, and sampling her warm and shamefully fragrant oils to relish the taste and flavour of sweet female sin.

As a result, I have to conclude that not only is it both easy and effective to chastise the female of the species in this way, it is also perfectly natural to enjoy it immensely. Mankind has never invented another pleasure so achingly complete.

The poetry of bottom smacking rhymes equally from her perspective also. To yield to your disciplinary will, she must present herself in the same head down, tail up position she would adopt to facilitate a vigorous and domineering sexual mount. Only in this case, she is offering her vulnerable end for the purposes of distressing torment rather than pleasurable copulation. This is obviously a far deeper submission than simply standing ready to be ridden, a degradation that adds to the ambience of humiliation and therefore greatly increases the value of the punishment.

I am a great fan of mother nature and her beautifully intricate wisdom, and when I take stock of the biological symmetry involved in spanking girls, and that undeniable yearning to whip their bottoms, rooted in my earliest memories of the opposite sex, I find it hard to believe that I am not somehow programmed in my DNA to beat the soft bare arse of my lover.

It is my predilection, my calling and my desire. It is why I am. Especially in the morning, when my dreams of her irresistible posterior charms retreat to the rock hard battlements of my awakening tower of manly lust.

She feels it, too: the deep instinctive rightness of a woman's sexual submission to the discipline of her man. She loves the powerful darkness of male control, manifest in his sadistic desire to hear her cry and whimper as he joyfully exploits the pretty weaknesses of her naked female form.

"Here is my bottom, spank me as hard as you will, Sir. I belong to you and I love you so. Please god, cleanse my tail end of its flammable wickedness with your wonderful sting, and make me yours again and again and again."

When I am whacking her, there is a consensual bond that is timeless, transcending the thousand generations spent forging the two opposite poles of our mutual fascination in the flames of sexual evolution.

Alpha to omega, top to bottom. Man to woman, palm to shivering cheek.

We are a rare breed we spankophiles. Like four leafed clovers, white tigers or blue whales. And as with other magnificent creatures so rarely seen in the wild, we are hidden from each other by the larger masses of vanilla boys and girls, and the secret nature of our kinky lust.

I grew up in simpler times, alone with my desires because I thought them to be uniquely mine. I took it for granted that I would never find a true mate, because my inner needs were so clearly not the norm, and no one else ever really talked about such things unless it was to deride the strangeness of such unusual sexual practice. Growing up, I felt guilt, loneliness and confusion.

But life and desire will always find a way, and through small moments of personal courage and many pleasing incidents of fortune, I found contact magazines and groups, and I saw that I was not alone and most exciting of all, it was not just a man thing!

Of course as time went by, and our wonderful society

became more tolerant, the books began to appear, and I felt no real shame, in fact a certain justification, in walking into a high street shop to buy a copy of the latest Silver Moon title. I felt rather liberated and proud to be part of a minority recognised by the enterprise of ingenious capitalists, writers, publishers and shopkeepers. It was a coming of age that I remember with great fondness.

Most fabulous of all though, was my discovery of the internet, when I found that we were not a few but many thousands all over the globe. Dominant men and submissive girls aplenty from Russia to the USA. A world within a world – and what a world! There are more pictures and mini movies of my favourite game out there than an excited and dedicated man could view in a breathless lifetime, and more pages dedicated to the spanker's art than my reeling brain can conceive, many of them compiled by wonderful girls.

So it is that technology has at last completed what nature had begun. Men who want to spank women, and women who want to be spanked, finally able to talk openly, to laugh, to meet and make good on the kinky promise burned deep into our secret sexual souls.

Now, I am no longer an aberration, but can relax and rejoice as just one of the crowd and celebrate the rightness of my deepest desires. I can be sure that it is not just wishful thinking, that nature does indeed have special secrets and I am lucky enough to know and feel this one in my heart, in my cock and in my bones.

My friends, you and I are blessed indeed.

So what happened next? I hear you ask. Having prised apart the lips of Pandora's punishment box, what spectacular disciplinary adventures led to the careful development of the thoroughly satisfying pastimes so lovingly described in this book?

I should very much like to share with you the highlights of my knee trembling journey through the secret pathways of dozens of submissive female bottoms, and the moist and yielding pussies that squirmed beneath them, as their owners' lithe bodies twitched in thrall to my sadistic amusement.

It will be my great pleasure to reveal the unbearably exciting details of these delicious exploits in volume II of this work: "The Whipping Girls"

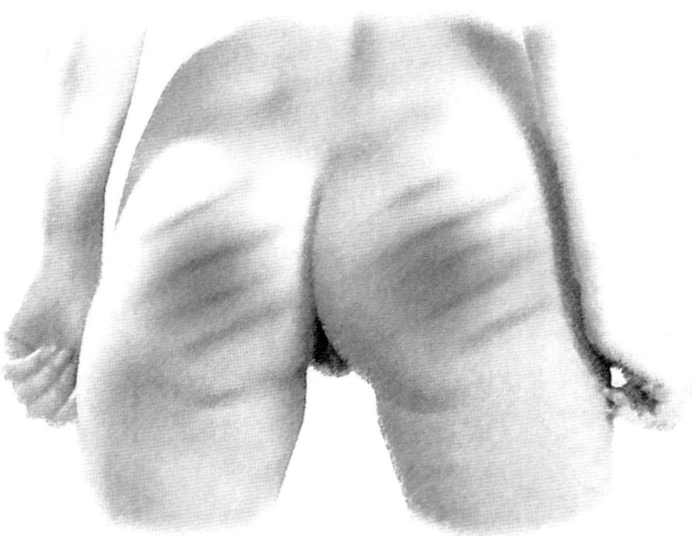

For sixteen years Silver Moon Books have carried the banner of BDSM onto the bookshelves of the nation – and not just this nation! - they are read and enjoyed worldwide and have devoted readership of both men and women who enjoy the delights that Peter has so eloquently described.

And in recent years we have also built up a mail order readership who appreciate the chance to browse and purchase at their leisure in the privacy of their own homes. But that's not all they get!

We frequently have promotions and special offers that are only open to mail order customers – who automatically and completely free of charge become Readers' Club Members. Via our bulletins they are told of super deals that can save them pounds and still provide them with their favourite authors' work and in some cases they can enjoy authors whose work is only available through mail order. For example:

REBECCA
GOOD BREEDING
THE APPRENTICE WHORE

All of these are by Katherine Forbes and are tales of harsh Victorian discipline that are immensely popular with our club members who appreciate the special chance to enjoy Katherine's unique talents.

And then there are the classics that have made Silver Moon such a famous name but which might not always be on the bookshelves near where you live. Francine Whittaker's knowing take on female submission is always a delight and can be sampled in;

THE CONNOISSEUR
PUNISHMENT BOUND
AMBER IN CHAINS
THE SLAVE PATH I, II AND III
THE WHIPMASTER
PLEASURE CONTROL
BRIDLED AND BOUND

Kim Knight is another lady who knows all about the delights of submission and her books are full of girl on girl as well as male dom action.

DARK SURRENDER
A SLAVE'S DESIRE
THE SLAVE HOUSE
THE CHAINS THAT BIND
THE MAKING OF A MISTRESS

Sean O'Kane's much praised Arena series is an imaginative and vivid saga of modern arenas where female gladiators are pitched against each other for the pleasure of their owners and the crowds. Brilliant scenes of flagellation and sex surround intricate sex scenes with page-turning plotlines.

INTO THE ARENA
THE GLADIATOR
THE PRIZE
SLAVE'S HONOUR
LAST SLAVE STANDING
GIRL SQUAD
NAKED AMBITION

New titles are added each month!

SilverMoon
Adult Fiction
Amber in Chains
Francine Whittaker

SM
SilverMoon
Adult Fiction
Bridled and Bound
Francine Whittaker

SM
SilverMoon
Adult Fiction
Into the Arena
an Arena novel
Sean O'Kane

SM
SilverMoon
Adult Fiction
Naked Ambition
Sean O'Kane

SM
SilverMoon
Adult Fiction
Pleasure Control
Francine Whittaker

Punishment Bound

Francine Whittaker

SM
SilverMoon
Adult Fiction
Slave's Honour
an Arena novel
Sean O'Kane

SM
Silver Moon
Adult Fiction
The Connoisseur
Francine Whittaker

SM
SilverMoon
Adult Fiction
The Gladiator
an Arena novel
Sean O'Kane